KU-353-235

AN AUSTRIAN AFFAIR

Lisa is a driver for her family firm, which runs coach tours abroad. On a trip to Austria, she meets Mark Treherne, who constantly asks questions about the company. She senses Mark is no ordinary tourist and feels he is reporting on her organisation. Later, when her father telephones to say they have been taken over by Treherne Holdings, Lisa bitterly confronts Mark. However, she has to apologise to him when she discovers her father's job is secure . . .

Books by Sheila Benton
in the Linford Romance Library:

MOUNTAIN LOVE

HANWORTH LIBRARY 10/05.

tw2 0 65 005

L.B. HOUNSLOW CIRCULATING COLLECTION	
SITE	DATE
1 HAN	09/05
2 Hou	01/07
3 Hes	10/08
4	
5	

Route 1 ✓

C0000 002 065 005

6

1

CHILDREN'S LIBRARY
CHISWICK LIBRARY H...

London Borough
of Hounslow

HAN

SPECIAL MESSAGE TO READERS

This book is published under the auspices of

THE ULVERSCROFT FOUNDATION

(registered charity No. 264873 UK)

Established in 1972 to provide funds for research, diagnosis and treatment of eye diseases. Examples of contributions made are: —

A Children's Assessment Unit at Moorfield's Hospital, London.

•

Twin operating theatres at the Western Ophthalmic Hospital, London.

•

A Chair of Ophthalmology at the Royal Australian College of Ophthalmologists.

•

The Ulverscroft Children's Eye Unit at the Great Ormond Street Hospital For Sick Children, London.

You can help further the work of the Foundation by making a donation or leaving a legacy. Every contribution, no matter how small, is received with gratitude. Please write for details to:

**THE ULVERSCROFT FOUNDATION,
The Green, Bradgate Road, Anstey,
Leicester LE7 7FU, England.
Telephone: (0116) 236 4325**

**In Australia write to:
THE ULVERSCROFT FOUNDATION,
c/o The Royal Australian and New Zealand
College of Ophthalmologists,
94-98, Chalmers Street, Surry Hills,
N.S.W. 2010, Australia**

SHEILA BENTON

---◆---

AN AUSTRIAN AFFAIR

Complete and Unabridged

LINFORD
Leicester

First published in Great Britain in 2004

First Linford Edition
published 2005

Copyright © 2004 by Sheila Benton
All rights reserved

British Library CIP Data

Benton, Sheila
An Austrian affair.—Large print ed.—
Linford romance library
1. Love stories
2. Large type books
I. Title
823.9′2 [F]

ISBN 1–84395–858–9

Published by
F. A. Thorpe (Publishing)
Anstey, Leicestershire

Set by Words & Graphics Ltd.
Anstey, Leicestershire
Printed and bound in Great Britain by
T. J. International Ltd., Padstow, Cornwall

This book is printed on acid-free paper

For Helen and Travis

1

The man swung round and caught her staring at him. Until that moment she'd seen only a side view of him as he stood, cup in hand, deciding where to sit. Idly she thought he looked interesting but when he turned and looked at the vacant seats at her table she was glad she was already sitting down.

Was he handsome? Could that be the reason she was so bowled over? Well, he certainly fitted the old cliché of tall, blonde and dashing. But mainly he was arresting. Yes, that was the word she was looking for. Well, he's certainly stopped me in my tracks she added to herself.

Dragging her eyes away, she concentrated on the coffee, stirring its sugarless depths while she sensed him moving nearer. The ferry lurched and instinctively she made a grab at the table as her coffee slithered and then stopped.

Oh, she wailed silently, please, not a choppy crossing.

Momentarily, her lashes hid the brown depth of her eyes and the bloom left her cheeks. Then running a hand through her long brown hair she squeezed her lids tightly shut and tried to pull herself together.

'The sea worries you?'

Her eyes snapped open and focussed on him. She'd been so bothered about the ship's motion she hadn't noticed he'd moved to sit opposite her.

'Oh, no,' she lied. 'I was just trying to save my coffee.'

Risking a glance at him, she saw that his eyes were taking in her workmanlike dark waistcoat and matching trousers, teamed with a cream shirt. Part of her resented his stare while the other half wished that she was wearing something more feminine.

A sudden pitch had her hands reaching out and clutching at the air until they were clasped by his.

'Your hands are freezing and you only just missed knocking my drink into my lap.'

His voice was deep with just a hint of a chuckle.

'I think you are more scared than you admit.'

'I just need time to get my sea legs, that's all.'

Angrily, she pulled her hands away. The man had been almost patronising. Well, perhaps he loved the sea, but she couldn't even swim. How could she expect to feel secure on a boat if she couldn't swim?

Leaning back, he studied her again and frowned at the severeness of her outfit which was so out of place among the casually-dressed holiday makers.

'Are you travelling alone?'

Now why should he assume she was by herself? She didn't like his question.

'No, I'm with a party of others. A coach party, actually.'

'Where to?'

He seemed intent on finding out her travel arrangements.

'Austria,' she replied abruptly.

'Really.'

'Why do you say really in that tone of voice?'

'Well,' his expression was amused as he looked once more at her attire.

'Well what?' she snapped.

There was something about him that irritated her.

'Just curious. You're not exactly dressed like the rest of us.'

'My clothes have nothing to do with you,' she said with more anger than intended.

'I beg your pardon?'

He scraped back his chair and rose to leave. Watching him stroll away as though the whole meeting had been unimportant to him, she felt a pang of regret. It would have been nice to while away the ferry trip in the company of a good-looking companion.

'I've brought more coffee and a packet of sugar. I don't know whether you take it.'

She hadn't noticed the stranger return and here he was sitting down opposite her again as though they were old friends.

'Oh, thank you,' she said lamely. 'Actually I don't take sugar.'

'At least now I know something about you, even if it's only that you don't take sugar. Perhaps we should introduce ourselves. Mark Treherne,' he said with a smile and rather formally he held out his hand across the table.

'Of course,' she almost stuttered, having trouble remembering her name. 'I'm Lisa, Lisa Browne, with an 'e',' she added automatically and held out her own hand.

He stroked her fingers.

'Hello, Lisa Browne, with an 'e'.'

He laughed softly as she pulled her hand away.

'So tell me about this holiday,' he said.

'I'm on a coach going to Austria. How about you?'

Quickly, she decided he didn't need

to know any more.

'That's where I'm going, too, just outside Salzburg.''

A little twinge of alarm rang in her ears. Surely he couldn't be going to the same place as herself. Was he travelling with them? Somehow she'd assumed he was alone. He didn't look as though he would enjoy a coach holiday.

'Yes, outside Salzburg,' he was still talking. 'It's an area I know well but I never tire of it and, of course, the city is beautiful. But this time I'm mixing business with pleasure.'

She raised her eyebrows, expecting him to enlarge upon the subject of his business, but he just said, 'A little research into a possible project.'

It was very obvious that he didn't want to talk about it.

Suddenly, she shivered, hoping that he wasn't on her tour. The crowd they had picked up all seemed very uncomplicated, just people intent on having a good time. No, he was definitely not the type to be on a coach holiday, she mused for in spite of his casual dress he was obviously successful. There was an aura around him, a confidence and certainty of his place in the world. Obviously he was more the type to fly and arrive quickly. Yes, he would be really out of place with them but she'd often found that people on holiday were full of surprises.

A couple passed their table and she caught the eye of her friend, Jane, passing behind Mark. She gave the thumbs-up sign to Lisa and rolled her eyes, her round face bright and happy as she pulled Andy, who had hesitated, away. Presumably she thought that Lisa wanted to be left alone with her companion.

She smiled at Jane's expression, knowing she would be cross-questioned about this when they next met. Watching them leave, she guessed they were making for the lounge area so at least she knew where her friends were if she wanted to join them.

'Do you always travel on a coach?'

she asked, turning her attention back to her companion and feeling in a happier mood.

'No, in fact,' he whispered conspiratorially, 'this is the first time.'

'They say there's a first time for everything.'

She laughed, thinking again that he just wouldn't fit in with the usual group and as though on cue, three young men passed, giving her friendly smiles.

'Are all these people friends of yours?' he asked.

'Oh, just part of the group. We only met today, of course, but they seem very nice.'

'Which company are you with?'

'Corane Tours,' she said casually.

'What a coincidence,' he said, leaning forward with a smile. 'So am I.'

'You weren't on the coach before.'

Her voice was almost accusing as she tried to work out if she was pleased or annoyed. There was no way she could have overlooked someone as attractive as he was.

Laughing at her surprise he added, 'I had business to attend to so I decided to join on the ferry crossing. In fact, my mother dropped me off. I might tell you,' he said confidingly, 'it was almost touch and go.'

'Touch and go?'

'Yes, I've known some terrible women drivers but my mother beats the lot, honestly.'

He appeared not to notice the change in the atmosphere. Clenching her hands, she counted silently to ten.

'That is remarkably unfair and old-fashioned. Also,' she added icily, 'statistics prove that women are a better insurance risk than men.'

His grin was mocking and suddenly she wondered if he was just winding her up and wasn't serious, but all at once she knew she had to get away from him. How could he sit there looking so self-satisfied and couldn't he sense how much she resented his attitude? Was he really so insensitive that he didn't notice the vibes she was sure were coming from her?

'In fact, I feel you're 'way behind the times.'

Her voice rose. That should do it! She was satisfied that she'd turned the tables on him, but he didn't even appear to hear her. Then he said the unforgettable and the completely unforgivable.

'Call me old-fashioned if you like, but I don't like being driven by a woman.'

This was terrible and getting worse by the moment. She had to get away, and fast.

'Excuse me,' she said and abruptly she stood up, almost knocking over her cup. 'I have to go.'

'Oh, I'm sorry.'

He rose quickly to his feet.

'Aren't you feeling too good? Is there anything I can do?'

'No, thank you,' she said through clenched teeth. 'I just have to go.'

'Oh, well, if you're all right. I'll see you on the coach.'

Obviously he was puzzled.

'Oh, no.'

Looking at her bewildered expression he probably thought she was some kind of maniac. Why else would she react so violently to the offer of company for the journey? Taking one last look into the brown eyes she almost ran, skirting the tables and the seemingly endless queue for snacks and made for the ladies' room. Leaning over the basin, she splashed her face and hands with cold water and took long, deep breaths. If only he wasn't travelling with them. The awful thing was that she couldn't afford to lose her temper with one of the party.

Just her luck, she thought again. He was the best-looking man she'd seen for ages and had appeared interested in her but it had gone badly from the start. Gathering up her things, she wondered where to go then began to see the funny side. Here she was, literally hiding in the ladies' like a schoolgirl. But of course there was Andy and Jane and there would be no need to spend any more time in the company of Mark Treherne, who teased her about women drivers and thought her clothes were a joke.

Entering the lounge area, she spotted her friends immediately. They were sitting close together and for a moment she hesitated, suddenly realising how friendly they'd become and wondered if something would develop between them during the next couple of weeks.

'Lisa,' Andy called over immediately and her problem was solved. 'Do you want something from the bar?'

He looked ruefully at the two glasses of orange juice in front of them as she sank on to the upholstered bench.

'No, thanks. I'm full right up with coffee.'

'Yes,' Jane joined in. 'Where did you find that gorgeous man?'

In spite of herself, she blushed when she saw the other girl's speculative look.

'I didn't find him. He sort of found me. That's all there was to it. We just shared a table for coffee.'

'He's on our tour,' Andy said, his blue eyes laughing. 'So things could start to happen.'

'That would be absolutely impossible. He informed me,' she announced dramatically, 'that he hates women drivers.'

Jane, who was sipping her drink, nearly choked and dissolved with laughter. Andy was grinning from ear to ear.

'It isn't that funny.'

Lisa tried to sound indignant but finally joined in.

'It'll be the biggest joke of the holiday,' Andy spluttered. 'Just wait until your dad hears about it.'

'Oh, let's change the subject. What do you think of the crowd, Jane?'

Sipping her drink, she took time replying.

'I reckon they'll be OK. I don't think any of them is the type to look for something to complain about, not like some runs. Do you remember that awful woman at the end of last year?'

The three, who had been together the previous season, were soon laughing as they recalled amusing instances. Then Lisa noticed that Jane was looking across at a point somewhere above her right shoulder and her spine started to tingle.

'May I join you?'

It was said casually enough and he was already seated before anyone could reply.

'Can I get you all a drink?'

He looked at Andy's unfinished glass of juice then seemed to notice that they were all wearing similar suits of waistcoat and trousers.

'Ah,' he said in satisfaction. 'I take it you're the crew.'

He laughed across to Andy.

'No wonder you're on soft drinks. You must be the driver.'

Lisa watched him as he completely took over the table. There was some-thing about his manner that stopped the lively conversation of a few minutes ago. Why had he come to join them? Hadn't she discouraged him sufficiently?

Turning to her, he smiled, as though they were on familiar terms and said, 'Perhaps you'll introduce me to your friends.'

Of course she would have introduced him. Did he think she was completely lacking in manners? He just hadn't given her time and now his attitude and tone of voice made her feel like a sulky schoolgirl. Trying not to show how annoyed she was at his intrusion, she made the introductions and sat back, determined not to take part in the conversation. She'd be polite but that's as far as it would go.

Her mind drifted to home and the problems her father was facing and then came back sharply as she heard Mark going over the itinerary with the other two. He was asking about the stopping places, the times and, of course, the route itself, all in so much detail that she began to wonder about him. Was he really just someone taking time off to relax on holiday?

'I'm sure you received our printed itinerary with your ticket,' she broke in icily, ignoring the startled looks of the others.

'Yes, I did.'

He turned to look at her.

'Then why all the questions?' she persisted.

Sitting back, he shrugged.

'I'm just one of those awkward people who likes to know everything.'

There was some light laughter but Lisa didn't join in. There was more to this man than was at first apparent, much more, she decided looking at him from under her lashes.

'Where do you pick up your extra driver?' he asked Andy.

'Driver?'

Andy's voice showed his surprise.

'No doubt we won't be travelling through to Austria with just one.'

Mark's voice had an edge to it.

'No, of course not. We have regulations and there are always two drivers. It's a long trip.'

16

Mark was now eyeing the girls.

'Two couriers also,' he drawled. 'Now that is a luxury. Tell me, do you take it in shifts or alternate days?'

He appeared not to notice the way Lisa sat up.

'How about the journey?' he continued. 'Does one of you cope with the day and one with the night as we're driving straight through?'

Lisa's colour rose. Had there been a slight innuendo in his voice or was it her imagination? It had become very quiet at the table and Jane, always sensitive to atmosphere, jumped up.

'Lisa are you ready? We'll be going down shortly,' she said and as she pushed past Andy she added, 'And you, come on it'll soon be time to go.'

Andy rose.

'You'll have to excuse us, Mark. Duty calls.'

He looked at Lisa who was still sitting.

'Coming or do you want to catch us up?'

'OK, Andy, I'll be with you in a moment.'

'I doubt we'll go without you anyway.'

Lisa grinned as the other two started to leave. There was something she wanted to say to this man, something that would put him in his place. Mark looked at her smiling face.

'Funny,' he said confidingly, 'it didn't dawn on me before that you were part of the team. Even seeing you in that uniform, it still didn't register that you were a courier.'

She opened her mouth to interrupt but he went on, 'Well, I warn you, I get bored very easily while I'm travelling and I shall expect a good commentary as we go. Another thing I like is lots of amusing detail about the places we travel through. I hope you've got plenty of interesting facts.'

Leaning forward slightly, she forced a smile and as she saw him stare at the opening at the neck of her shirt, she leaned forward even farther.

'I'm afraid I don't do a commentary,' she said softly.

'Oh, why is that?'

Sitting back abruptly, she stuck her chin in the air and said frostily, 'I am not your courier.'

'Presumably you do something or you wouldn't be in that uniform.'

He smiled.

'Oh, I admit you're very decorative but surely you're not here for the ride or something for us to look at when the scenery gets boring.'

Anger welled up as she looked him straight in the eyes.

'I do have my own position with the company,' she said coldly.

His mouth twitched.

'Well, if you're not a courier, what are you?'

She stood up and had the advantage of looking down at him.

'Your driver, Mr Treherne. I am your driver.'

2

Lisa didn't dare wait to see Mark's expression change but, heart thudding, she whirled and fled. If only she could catch her friends she would feel safe from his dominating presence but the other two had a few minutes' start.

She couldn't explain the need to run from him which was impossible because there was nowhere to go. He was travelling with her and not only today to Austria but throughout the whole of the holiday and the journey home. Day after day of his company looked like a dark cloud on her horizon. Sighing softly, she shrugged, knowing that she couldn't afford the luxury of being upset.

For a while, she quickened her steps. The fact that there was a passenger on their coach who had no confidence in her ability had to be put to one side.

She mustn't brood about it and imagine him watching the road and waiting for her to take the wrong direction. Oh, well, she shrugged, at least I'm sharing with Andy so I'll be able to spend a little time in peace.

As she reached the distinctive blue and white coach, Jane was standing at the automatic door waiting for the passengers.

'Come on, Lisa, I began to think you'd been abducted,' she teased.

Andy was inside, fiddling around with the video machine that had caused so much trouble last year. She gave him a sympathetic look as she slipped into the driving seat knowing they ought to invest in a new one but it all came back to money.

'I think it will hold out.'

He stacked up the cassettes, choosing a couple of films.

'Let's hope that if it gives up, everyone will have dropped off to sleep and they won't notice.'

'Quick,' Jane said under her breath as

she glanced at their worried faces. 'Plaster on the smiles, here come the first passengers. At least they look healthy enough.'

She grimaced.

'I don't think anyone was actually sick on the crossing.'

'I was pretty queasy at the start,' Lisa said, 'but when the wind dropped it wasn't too bad, so I reckon they'll be OK.'

Jane was in her element, asking everyone if they'd enjoyed the crossing. She really was a lovely person. Lisa looked at the other girl, envying the cheerful friendliness that was entirely natural. She hesitated only once and that was when Mark stepped quickly inside.

'Hello, again, Mark. You're our new passenger, aren't you?'

She smiled, consulting her list.

'Ah, yes, here you are, Mark Treh-erne.'

Lisa's heart fell as she heard the words, 'Right up here in the front, you are. You'll have an excellent view.'

The double seat right behind the driver was always kept for the other crew members but directly across the aisle and almost right beside them, Mark was already dumping his jacket. What rotten luck! It was always unfortunate to have someone awkward at the front with them, but perhaps the other two wouldn't think he was difficult.

Already Jane was chatting away to him quite happily and what's more, he was responding. Trying to make it appear causal, Lisa risked a glance over her shoulder. She need not have worried. He wasn't looking in her direction but was now stretching up to stow his hand luggage in the locker above the seat.

Her eyes lingered and once again she noticed the breadth of his shoulders and the strong muscles as he lifted what appeared to be a heavy bag. Swiftly realising the train of her thoughts, she swivelled in her seat and looked straight ahead.

Her back was strained and rigid as she wriggled to get comfortable but today the seat didn't feel right and every control appeared to be in the wrong position. Squeezing her eyes shut, she tried to push away the thought that she wasn't going to cope. A tight band was wrapping itself around her head with the beginnings of a head-ache. When someone tapped her on the shoulder, she jumped, afraid to glance round but it was only Andy.

'You look a bit uptight,' he whispered. 'Want me to do the first bit? It won't matter if we swap.'

Knowing she was a coward, she let the weakness sweep over her. It was against all her principles and she knew she was backing down, but it was a lifeline and she took it.

'Thanks, Andy. I'm OK really, but that would be brilliant. There's been a lot of worry at home, as you know. It's been a bit traumatic but I'll be all right soon and we can change back at the first stop.'

'That's fine.'

He squeezed her shoulder as she slid from the seat. As though it had been pre-arranged, he casually took her place, turning sideways to join Jane in greeting the last few people in the group. Without looking in the direction of Mark and keeping her eyes straight ahead, she walked down the aisle to the drinks machine.

'Any chance of a beer?' one of the young men teased as he made his way to his seat.

'Tea, coffee and orange juice, much better for you,' she teased back.

There was some good-natured grumbling among the lads as she unpacked a new box of plastic cups, stacking them and neatly checking until she heard the swish of the doors and knew they were on their way.

Dropping momentarily into a spare seat, she listened with the others while Jane described the journey. She apologised for the arrangement of a meal stop which was very late but advised everyone to take advantage of the break to have some food.

'Why was it arranged so late?'

The voice, of course, belonged to Mark.

'We do have to fit in with the times of the ferry,' Jane replied as she smiled at him. 'Does it bother you to eat late?'

Well done, Lisa thought. Jane had handled it beautifully and with a lovely smile. Leaning slightly outwards, Lisa looked at the first row of seats. It was worse than she'd expected, for Mark was sitting alone and it now seemed unlikely anyone else would join them so he would have a seat to himself. She bit her lip as she thought about the implications. A seat to himself meant that he wouldn't have a companion to chat to and take up his attention. He was free to concentrate on the crew. But maybe he would settle down and behave like a normal person on holiday.

'When do we get our first beer?'

The young men were just behind and they teased and chatted, obviously delighted to have her among them. While she joined in with her own line of backchat, she tried to keep the noise down as their young laughter rang out. But it was a losing battle and when, after a time, she noticed a few heads turning in her direction, she tossed a casual, 'See you later,' over her shoulder to them and stood up.

Knowing that Jane was at the end of her talk and about to sit down, Lisa slid into the seat behind Andy. Her timing was perfect for, as she took the window side, Jane flopped into the aisle seat which was just across from Mark. Now Lisa was effectively shielded from him.

Andy put a tape in the player and low background music to a film drifted over them. At the same time a general buzz of conversation broke out amongst the various groups.

Certain that any conversation would be lost in the general noise, Jane asked in a low voice, 'What gives with you and this Mark? I thought it all looked very cosy on the boat but now you're ignoring each other so pointedly I'm getting certain vibes. Have you had a row with him already?'

'He is the most rude, irritating man I've ever met and the less I have to do with him the better.'

'Tell me more,' Jane teased. 'Are you sure you're not the tiniest bit interested in him?'

Lisa's colour rose.

'Definitely not. How could I be when he's got this hang-up about women drivers?'

With the frankness of a firm friendship, Jane said, 'Aren't you taking this a bit too seriously? A lot of men go on about women drivers. I can't see why you're in such a state. Frankly you look awful.'

'I can't explain even to myself why I'm so bothered. It was the way he said it, I suppose, or maybe it's me being extra sensitive.'

'Is that why Andy's taken over?'

'Only until we have a stop. He just thought I looked a bit fraught.'

'And you certainly are. Does this Mark know that he's upsetting the boss's daughter?'

'Huh, he wouldn't care. By the look of him, he could buy us three times over.'

Leaning across, she risked a glance at the subject of their conversation. He had a briefcase on his knees and was looking through some papers. The thought occurred to her how strange he looked when most of the party were engrossed in magazines or looking at the film. Turning back to Jane, she continued.

'I don't know why he's on this tour at all. I'm sure it's not his sort of thing. Just look at his clothes and general attitude. He could afford something much better than this cut-price holiday.'

'Don't knock it,' Jane said and touched her friend's hand. 'It's a jolly good holiday and a lot of people are glad to take it. I haven't liked to ask lately, but how are things now?'

Worry clouded Lisa's face.

'Just about the same when I left,' she replied. 'The trouble now is that we're just not making a profit but have actually started to lose money, only a little, but definitely a downward trend.'

'It's as bad as that?'

Lisa knew Jane was probably thinking about her own job. Although she didn't want to cause her friend any more worry she just had to talk to someone and if everything went badly they would soon know anyway. Lisa's face was strained.

'We never have made much money, just enough to keep us ticking over. Then last year we just about broke even but so far this year we've lost some money and Dad's worried out of his mind.'

'What about the people who were interested in taking you over?'

Jane glanced quickly around to check they weren't being overheard.

'Their accountant was going over the books as I left.'

'What was he like? Did he give you

any idea if they're going to carry on with the bid?'

'Nice enough person,' she answered. 'Quite young really. Dad took to him, I could see that. Well, I thought he was OK, too.'

Jane's normal, lively expression was pensive.

'When will you know?' she asked.

'About a couple of weeks. Jane, I shouldn't worry you with our problems. I know you're thinking about your job. You and Andy have worked so hard and I can't bear to think it could be for nothing.'

She swallowed hard, clenching her hands.

'I've been so worried since I left home that I've barely been able to think straight. It's hard to keep it all to myself and put a good face on things.'

'I know what you mean. This is a holiday and we should be keeping the atmosphere light and happy. Don't worry about Andy and me. You know we're right behind you.'

'Not behind me,' she said giving her a sweet and grateful smile. 'You're both beside me and thanks for listening. Now, I've just got to think of making the tour a success.'

They both became quiet, busy with their own thoughts. Lisa dozed lightly. The chat with Jane had done her good. Just airing her problems had eased the pressure which had threatened to overwhelm her all day.

A slight jolt and Jane's voice brought her awake as she realised they were at their first stopping point. While most passengers stretched their legs she leaned over Andy.

'It's OK, I'll take over now.'

He nodded and once again they changed places. The rest had cleared her head and her confidence had returned. Most of the returning passengers gave her a quick smile and a couple of younger girls gave her a thumbs-up sign as they noticed the change of drivers. As a pair of wide shoulders filled the doorway, she deliberately looked Mark in the eye daring him to move a muscle in his face or even say a word. But his face was expressionless. After a quick head count, Jane gave a nod. The automatic doors closed and the engine throbbed into life powerfully. They were off.

Time sped by, broken only by the lights of other vehicles. A quick glance at the clock told her they were approaching a service station and she welcomed the break. Here she could get a meal and then make for the small sleeping compartment in the lower part of the coach.

'I'll take care of the fuel.'

Andy's voice made her jump.

'We're locking up so you can leave things in the coach but be sure to be back here in one hour,' Jane said, calm, fresh and unflappable as she made her announcement and Lisa envied her matter-of-fact attitude.

Passing her at the door Lisa whispered, 'I'll save you a place at my table.'

The two girls exchanged grins. This

was one of their favourite stops with a good variety of food and time to chat and swap news about the passengers. Jumping lightly from the coach, Lisa quickly made her way through the darkened area to the brightly-lit restaurant. Another tour operator had stopped and there were people everywhere. Quickly she joined the mass of people waiting and gathered up a roll, coffee and salad. Not wanting to appear unsociable, she searched around for a vacant table.

She'd been waiting for this for several hours and for a moment she slumped in her seat with her hands inelegantly around the warmth of her cup. She hadn't noticed anyone coming until a plate of steaming food was placed opposite her. She shuddered, wondering who could consume so much at such an unearthly hour. She raised her eyes and there was Mark. He was even smiling down at her as he pulled out a chair.

'Don't mind if I join you?'

Without waiting for an answer he sat

and started on his meal.

'You drive well,' he said after a few minutes.

Startled, she looked up while the words took time to sink in. Even then she expected to see a sarcastic gleam in his eyes but what she saw was pure sincerity.

'Er . . . thank you,' she muttered, blushing like a teenager.

'Look, I reckon I spoke out of turn back there on the ferry.'

He had the grace to look embarrassed.

'You sounded as though you meant every word,' she snapped, spearing a piece of tomato as though it were him.

'I admit I'm prejudiced about lady drivers but I've never actually come across your kind of professional female driver before.'

It began to sound a little less like an apology and she glared across at him as her temper rose with every word.

'As I say,' he continued, 'these circumstances are exceptional.'

'So you take it all back?' she questioned sharply, determined not to give way.

He ran a hand through his hair causing it to flop across his forehead.

'Well?' she repeated briskly, forcing herself not to come under his charm. 'Do you take it back?'

'You haven't seen my mother at the wheel,' he said ruefully, 'or you wouldn't ask.'

'That's still no reason to be so prejudiced against us all.'

'OK. I take your point.'

He reached forward and took both her hands in his.

'These two small hands have a terrific responsibility. That's a big coach for a woman. No rings?'

There was a pause while she gathered her thoughts. Her single state was nothing to do with him.

'That means nothing these days,' she retorted, 'nothing at all.'

'I noticed you enjoyed the company of those young boys at the back when we started off. I thought you made quite a din down there.'

'Just youthful high spirits.'

She made it sound as though she thought he was Methuselah and he was aware of it. She could tell by the quick frown and narrowing of the eyes.

'I'm not in my dotage, you know,' he said eventually.

'I'm sure it couldn't matter less,' she said casually. 'I'm sure you don't have to prove anything to me. After this holiday we'll never see each other again.'

She wrapped her uneaten roll in a paper serviette.

'Now if you'll excuse me I've got some sleep to catch up on.'

She left the table before he could reply and walked away quickly.

'For someone who hates a certain man, you spend a lot of time with him.'

It was Jane, her voice mocking but at the same time slightly suspicious.

'I'm sorry, Jane. I kept you a seat and suddenly he was there.'

'I think that something is developing between you two. He's got a definite appeal or why else are you always sharing a table?'

'There's only one thing that appeals to me right now and that's a good sleep. Tell Andy to drive gently. I need my rest.'

As she tried to settle in the small space, she unwrapped her roll and bit on it savagely. Why couldn't the man leave her alone?

The swaying of the coach soon told her they were on their way again and she resolved that once they arrived in Austria she would do everything in her power to avoid Mark.

3

At the next stop, Lisa wriggled from her compartment and, hoping no-one was watching, ran to the ladies' room. Pulling out her toothbrush, she followed her usual routine of cleaning her teeth and quickly washed her hands and face. Time was limited but she managed to renew her make-up and flick her hair into place. The responsibility of the last part of the journey was hers and now she was ready to change places again with Andy.

There was just time for a breakfast roll and coffee from the cafeteria which was fairly empty. The majority of travellers were walking around to stretch their cramped limbs. Sipping her drink, she grimaced slightly and looked forward to her next cup which should be the thick, Austrian variety she loved. Checking her watch, she swallowed the remainder knowing time was getting short and that as a member of the crew she couldn't keep the coach waiting.

Reaching the coach, she was relieved to find that it wasn't quite full and as she sprang up the steps she came face to face with Mark.

'You look more lifelike,' he said with a grin.

Her temper rose and then subsided as she saw the funny side.

'Did you see me crawling out of my hole?'

'Yes, like a small snail leaving the comfort of her shell.'

The words were ordinary but some-how they spread over her like a caress. His eyes twinkled with humour and suddenly she was looking at him in a new way. She guessed that he could, if he tried, be a very pleasant companion, only he didn't try very often where she was concerned.

'At least I was able to sleep lying down. I know what it's like spending the night sitting up even if the seats do recline slightly. It's not very comfortable.'

'It's not my favourite mode of travel but at least I've got plenty of room up here in the front. I'm not too cramped. That was one of the reasons I asked to be put there.'

'One of the reasons,' she questioned frowning. 'Were there others?'

'Obviously I like to see where I'm going,' he replied casually, almost too casually.

'Any other reason?'

While trying to keep her voice light and casual she managed to study his expression, but his face was impassive and he obviously had no intention of answering her question. Wishing now that she hadn't questioned him she moved slightly and her leg brushed his knee, causing her to step away abruptly. Why had she over-reacted to something that was always happening? He must think her a gauche schoolgirl. She wouldn't look at him as she thought he might be laughing at her and so her eyes dropped to the empty space beside him.

Instead of the usual holiday clutter spread over the seat, there were business-type papers and a lap-top computer. Aware that her leg still tingled and to get over the awkward moment she spoke rather abruptly.

'Do you always bring your work with you?'

Looking at her levelly he replied, 'Only when it's necessary.'

'And it is at the moment?'

'Yes, very.'

She felt he was reading her mind as he added, 'What a lot of questions you ask.'

This was getting her nowhere and she snapped.

'Are you really so indispensable?'

'Of course,' his eyes glittered dangerously. 'Aren't you?'

She was stumbling on difficult ground and with a small smile she turned away and put an end to the conversation. By the time the remaining passengers arrived she was sitting at the wheel looking pretty and fresh with her back straight and confident.

The miles flew by as the scenery changed from endless main highways to a slower, more interesting route. Chalet-type houses started to appear and in the distance were green, pine-covered slopes as they made their way towards the mountains of Austria. Only another hour, she reckoned, and they would be there.

The journey hummed on uneventfully and when Jane began talking to the party again they were pulling into the space at the side of the hotel. Lisa sat for a time flexing her back while Jane saw everyone off with their belongings. Andy was already at the luggage compartment and some young lads were coming out to help carry in the cases.

By the time she entered the lobby, most of the group had been allocated their rooms and she waited with Jane and Andy until everyone had gone. Looking around, she tried to get the feel of the place. This was a hotel they hadn't used before but the atmosphere was friendly and welcoming. In isolated splendour, it stood on high ground above the village.

After the few greetings and formalities had been completed, the three of them were led along a hallway on the ground floor.

'Three in a line,' Jane giggled as first Andy, then herself and lastly Lisa were given their single rooms. 'I'm for kicking off my shoes and having a rest. See you at dinner, OK?'

'OK,' Lisa agreed, looking forward to being on her own for a time.

Dumping her bag she made for the balcony, opening the doors and gulping great breaths of clear air. Thank goodness the place had plenty of single rooms. This was her very own for the next ten days. She could read all night or play her radio quietly. Turning back into the room, the pristine white duvet and pillows looked so soft and inviting that she decided on a quick shower and a rest before dinner.

She awoke to the sound of someone moving in the next room. For a moment she was disorientated thinking it was Jane but the sounds were from the opposite wall, right behind her bed. Glancing at her watch she was horrified to see how long she'd slept and mentally thanked the unknown occupant for waking her.

Swinging her feet to the floor she thought rapidly about what she should wear for the evening. Eventually she chose a simple dress in swirls of grey and deep pink. It was so good to be out of her uniform.

As she left her room, the door of the neighbouring room opened and immaculate in dark slacks and blazer stood Mark. Her smile of welcome disappeared along with the friendly greeting that seemed to be stuck in her throat. He was the last person she expected to see and it threw her completely.

Frantically she looked along the hallway but both Jane's and Andy's doors were firmly shut. As much as she hated the idea, there was nothing for it but to walk with him to the dining-hall. All the same she couldn't help wondering about his well-groomed good looks. His clothes were well-cut and obviously expensive in an understated way and once again she puzzled why anyone who could afford to dress in such a manner chose this particular holiday. Was there indeed some mystery here or was her imagination working overtime?

'Are you tired from the journey?' she asked politely.

He flexed his shoulders.

'More stiff than tired. Trying to sleep on a coach isn't exactly my idea of comfort.'

She raised her eyebrows.

'Why opt for that kind of travel? There are other means of holiday transport and you have a choice. Why did you pick this particular holiday?'

'Do you cross question all your clients in this way?'

'Only people who don't seem to fit

46

in,' she said and then wondered if she'd gone too far.

But for a change he looked slightly disconcerted.

'I'll try anything once. Fortunately I'm the type who doesn't need a lot of sleep.'

No, she thought, he wouldn't and was glad she hadn't had that bit of information during her night-time drive. The idea of him being the only passenger awake through the long hours would have been a severe strain on her concentration.

'What's the problem with your video on the coach? I noticed it seemed about to give up.'

Blast the man! Why couldn't he sleep like everyone else instead of noticing when the machine had played up?

'Perhaps it was the conditions,' she said blithely. 'We don't always get a perfect reception when we're travelling.'

'I don't think that was the trouble.'

Was she imagining a slight menace in his tone? She quickened her steps, anxious to be away from him. Of course, she should have known better.

There was no way she would be able to outstride him and he was beside her again.

'Have you had it long?'

'What?'

'The video,' he persisted. 'Have you had it long? It seems to be an old model.'

'I really couldn't tell you,' she lied. 'In any case, what does it matter if it is an old model?'

'Nothing,' he said smoothly, 'as long as it works but this one doesn't seem to work very well.'

'In your brochure,' she said icily, 'there is a section for any complaints you may wish to make. Perhaps you would care to enter your comments about the video recorder.'

Luckily, they reached the dining-hall which put an end to their rather stilted conversation and she quickly walked to the table reserved for the tour staff. Mark, she was pleased to see, was shown to a place well away from her. She did, however, wonder who his dinner companions would be and hoped they would be able to put up with his rather high-handed attitudes.

'Hmm,' Jane drawled as she sat down, her eyes twinkling. 'With Mark again, I notice.' Trying to keep a straight face she continued, 'He is the one person on this holiday whom you totally and utterly dislike, isn't he?'

Lisa flushed with confusion, and then remembered this was Jane she was with, one of her closest friends.

'He is a spy, Jane, I'm sure of it. He was asking how long we've had the video recorder. It was as though he knew we couldn't afford to replace it.'

Jane reached across and touched her arm with sympathy.

'Don't worry too much. You may have the wrong idea. If he is, there is nothing you can do about it and we must concentrate on the rest of the people and make sure they have a good time.'

At that moment, Andy joined them and the meal passed happily enough.

Now and again she caught Mark's eye as though he was staring a lot in her direction. She giggled slightly to herself as she saw the young men being shown to the empty seats at his table, the same young men he'd found boisterous when she'd sat at the back of the coach with them. Serve him right for criticising the noise they'd made!

Sensing that Jane and Andy wanted to be alone, she refused their offer to join them in an after-dinner stroll and watched them walk away. Feeling lost, she wondered where to go. The sensation of being conspicuously alone was a new one, but she would look on it as a challenge. She would be independent and buy herself a drink from the bar. Suddenly the idea of a cool glass of white wine was very appealing, and she headed for the bar.

'Hi.'

Twisting round, glass in hand, she saw two young girls from the coach beckoning to her. Thankfully she moved over to them and pulled out a stool.

Sara and Jo were so uncomplicated and outgoing that she soon relaxed in their company. She accepted their compliments on her ability to drive such a large vehicle and, combined with the wine, this soon had her telling them hilarious stories of her lessons when she was learning to handle such a monster. Soon the girls began to discuss the rest of the party.

'There are a few quite good-looking men which should help the holiday along,' Jo said cheekily.

'Oh, the ones at the back of the coach are just right for you two, I should imagine,' she teased.

'And how about you?' Jo said. 'We must find someone for you.'

'Oh, I don't need anyone. You forget, I'm working.'

'But we all need someone to share the evenings with. How about the guy at the front?' Sara said.

Lisa frowned as though she had no idea whom she meant.

'Which one?' she replied.

'Don't tell me you haven't noticed.'

She watched Lisa who flushed slightly.

'He's slightly older and travelling alone. You know, the one with the self-assured manner and expensive clothes. No warm-blooded woman could fail to notice him. In fact, Jo and I thought you quite fancied him.'

'Why should you think that? Quite frankly,' she confided, 'I've spoken to him a couple of times and he is certainly not my type.'

The last thing in the world she wanted was anyone speculating about her and Mark. The idea was ridiculous and she had enough to worry about without that. Half an hour later she said her good-nights and headed back to her bedroom.

Opening her balcony doors, she gazed out at the night. It was breath-taking. Looking down the valley she could see the lights of the tiny village looking like so many stars. Down there would be people drinking and singing in the beer-garden but up here, with the tree-covered slopes of the mountain behind them, it was quiet and peaceful.

For a moment, an ache of loneliness surged through her. This year, she realised, as kind as her colleagues were, she was going to be the odd one out. During the days she would be well occupied but there was no getting away from the fact that her evenings could be solitary. She had to face it, unless she became friendly with some of the others on the tour, she'd be spending a lot of time in her own company.

Just then, a movement on the adjoining balcony caught her eye and she wondered who else was looking at the night. Then it hit her with the force of a hammer. Of course, it was Mark. She cursed petulantly. Just knowing he was there spoiled the peace of the evening. Why hadn't he gone to the village with the young men from his table? Then she smiled in gentle satisfaction. They probably thought he was too old!

Feeling suddenly tired, she undressed quickly and sank into bed. The night was quiet. Not a sound came from the adjoining rooms and then a bed creaked as though a heavy body was lowered on to it.

'Mark,' she muttered, sitting up abruptly and then heard the groan of her own bed, deafening in the silent room. Suddenly she realised that due to the positioning of the rooms, their beds were one each side of a dividing wall.

She'd never be able to relax. There was nothing for it but to ask for a different room, she decided, but what reason could she give? Absolutely none. If it was Jane or a stranger that she could hear she wouldn't give it another thought. It was because it was Mark. She'd only known him a short time and he was already disturbing her.

Tensing her body, she tried not to make a sound as she wriggled deeper under the duvet and willed herself to lie rigid and wide-eyed in the darkness.

She looked at the wall, feeling certain that if she reached out she could touch him. Impulsively, she stretched out her arm thinking it might be nice to find him near, to reach out to him in the darkness of the Austrian night.

4

The village lay in a pool of early-morning light and the pretty, flower-decked houses floated as on a silver, shimmering lake. Thank goodness she was alone, for any company would detract from the beauty of the scene. Lisa was up early and hoped to be the first one to leave the hotel. Surprisingly she had slept soundly at last and woken refreshed.

Dressed in jeans and T-shirt in toning blues she had casually knotted the arms of a soft cream sweater around her shoulders and crept outside. Her feet slithered as the hillside steepened. Half running the last few yards, she reached level ground.

'It's beautiful, isn't it?'

'The most beautiful place in the world. I call it fairyland,' she answered still in her trance.

Seconds later, her mood broke as twisting swiftly she saw that she was no longer alone. Today Mark was in black jeans and sweater. The total effect managed to be both casual and dramatic.

'It seems that we've found a subject on which we can agree at last.'

His gentle smile was at odds with the rather formal words.

For a time they talked leisurely, drawn together by their mutual appreciation of the beauty before them. The tiny shaft of anger that she was no longer alone briefly welled up and just as quickly fled. His presence enhanced rather than spoiled her mood. Incredibly they were enjoying each other's company.

He took her hand as they scrambled down to the tiny stream and she was content to leave her fingers curled within his grasp. Then all at once she felt trapped. It was all changing too fast. Yesterday she hated and almost feared this man and now new but just as compelling feelings were overtaking her. The sensation of her hand in his was too pleasant, too right and she tore herself from his grasp, going down on her knees and plunging her fingers into the running water. Shuddering she swiftly withdrew her hand, shaking off the icy droplets.

'I never remember how cold these streams are. Every year I get caught.'

Her voice was uneven as she tried to bring it under control.

He glanced upwards.

'This probably comes straight off the mountain and you can see how cold it is up there.'

'Stupid of me to forget,' she murmured almost unaware of her words and she stood up reaching just to his shoulder.

'Is this your day off?' he asked.

'No, just the morning. There's a tour of the lake this afternoon as we stop for cake at . . . '

'Oh, spare me the full itinerary.'

He laughed and two pairs of

sparkling eyes locked together, darkened and became serious with awareness. He moved nearer, his head lowering and she knew he was going to kiss her. His lips softened, parted and waited. Then at the corner of her eye she saw a couple of people coming towards them and the moment was broken. Swinging round she started to make her way back to a bridge over the stream. There was now a number of people strolling around and the place was no longer her own to enjoy.

'You don't like crowds?'

He was close to her again.

'I must admit I do like this place to myself. Selfish, I know, but it's why I was down here early.'

'And did I spoil it for you?'

'No, you didn't. I wouldn't like you to think that.'

'I'm glad,' he said simply, taking her hand and they walked on in silence.

She hadn't expected to enjoy sharing her early-morning walk but somehow everything had been heightened with his presence. Glancing swiftly at him she asked herself if she wanted to get involved with Mark. A sixth sense told her that if she let herself like him too much she would never want to get away.

'I'm going up above the village to take pictures. You'll come with me?'

It was more of a statement than a question but she didn't resent it and was content to walk beside him. For the first time, she noticed the expensive camera slung over his shoulder and was glad she'd left her basic model in her room. When they reached the top of the incline he spoke casually.

'I understand your father owns Corane Tours.'

'Where did you hear that?'

One eyebrow was raised in amusement at her outburst.

'Is it highly-classified information?'

He made it sound as though her angry reaction had been ridiculous.

'I . . . er . . . usually keep it to myself

otherwise I would be bombarded with suggestions and complaints,' she said stiffly. 'It would make my job unbearable to be known as the boss's daughter.'

'Of course, of course. I understand.'

He patted her shoulder as though she were a small girl who'd just got over a temper tantrum and all the pleasure of the morning evaporated.

'You mentioned complaints,' he said almost to casually. 'Do you get many?'

What a fool she'd been to let her tongue run away with her.

'Complaints? Can't think why I said that,' she said, her laugh forced and high. 'Rarely do we have a complaint. We try to give absolute satisfaction.'

'Hey, slow down. I wasn't suggesting anything.'

Now the morning was spoiled and as he took photographs, she pondered over who had told him about her father. How did he know?

She was quiet as they walked back to the hotel. The more she turned things over in her mind, the more her suspicion grew. Could he, in fact, be connected with the take-over? Someone could have telephoned him or he could have made a call. The more she considered the idea, the more logical it became.

'Coffee?'

So engrossed was she in her thoughts that she jumped and looked vaguely at him.

'Oh, no, thank you,' she said quickly. 'I've some checking to do for this afternoon.'

Was it her imagination or did he look disappointed? Turning as though making for her room, once she was out of sight she turned and walked swiftly to the reception area.

With her words silently rehearsed, she approached the desk in what she hoped to be a casual manner. The young man, who introduced himself as Steffan, eyed her appreciatively and she knew that gave her an advantage. With just the right amount of indifference in her voice, she inquired about calls to the United Kingdom and asked the charges.

'I don't suppose anyone has made any calls yet,' she asked.

'A couple,' he replied. 'People want their families to know they have arrived safely, you understand.'

'And then hope they leave them alone and don't ring back here,' she joked giving him a wide smile.

He was so intent on watching her face that he didn't answer.

'I don't suppose that's happened yet,' she carried on, laughing lightly.

He was completely thrown off guard.

'Only last night I was on duty when a call came through for Mr Treherne.'

Perhaps it was her gasp that made him realise that he should not be talking about another guest at the hotel and he stopped abruptly. She shrugged, trying to put him at his ease.

'Just wondering who'd want to bother.'

She hoped he would be dazzled again

by her smile into divulging the name of the other party but he clammed up.

Well, she thought it was worth a try and anyway she knew now that Mark had received a call from home. Instantly she was desperate to know the answers but there was nothing more she could do. To confront Mark would be to put him on his guard. No, she would watch and listen. A brilliant idea flashed into her mind and swiftly she made her way to her room.

Reaching into her bag, she pulled out a new notebook. On the front page she wrote MARK TREHERNE, then underneath, **Who is he**? Then she sat on the bed and tried to remember every conversation they'd had and every remark he'd made which she thought could be suspect. Excitedly she made notes, starting with his dislike of women drivers. Why did he criticise the video recorder asking how old it was and how frequently it broke down? Had he deliberately sought her out this morning to gain more information?

She hated writing the last point and hoped it wasn't true but if it was she would have to face the fact that it wasn't her charms that won him but the knowledge that she was her father's daughter. Casting her mind back, she was surprised at the small details she remembered, even his query about the late meal-stop and the way he'd almost pounced at her mention of complaints. Hopefully a picture of what Mark Treherne was up to would emerge. She wrote rapidly, covering several pages.

At last she sat back and looked at her scrawl. Was she letting her fancy run away with her or were the notes a record of true and more sinister facts!

The morning had somehow flashed past and, splashing her face with cold water, she tried to relax and gather her thoughts for the afternoon. Putting on her uniform, she took a cool look at herself in the mirror. Actually she admitted, the tailored lines of the outfit flattered her figure. The waistcoat nipped into her small waist and the trousers fitted neatly over her hips. Outlining her mouth with a brighter than usual lipstick she sternly told herself to enjoy the opportunity that brought her to this lovely place and not allow anyone to spoil it for her. In a lighter mood, she sauntered along the corridor and into reception.

A crowd had already gathered and she chatted to one or two people, answering questions before shepherding them out to the waiting coach. Andy was already at the wheel.

'Have you got the details of where we're going? I want to hear that commentary loud and clear,' he joked.

'I've got it all up here,' she answered and tapped her forehead. 'I've also got some leaflets to hand out which will keep everyone occupied.'

She shuffled the papers from her briefcase into neat piles. She always enjoyed herself when Jane had time off, deciding that to be a courier was far less taxing on the nervous system than being a driver.

Immediately she began counting heads she noticed the empty front seat. Thank goodness she would be spared the worrying of watching Mark this afternoon.

'We appear to be one short,' she told the passengers. 'Anyone hiding under the seats?'

There was some polite laughter at this old, familiar joke. Hopefully he wouldn't be coming. Then Jo called from the back.

'Mark's coming. We saw him a few minutes ago, didn't we, Sara?'

'Yes, that's right,' Sara joined in. 'Mustn't go without him, must we?'

In spite of her resolutions, Lisa felt herself flushing. Embarrassment made her voice brisk.

'We can't hold up the coach for one person.'

Just then, he appeared, taking the two steps in one long stride.

'Sorry,' he muttered. 'I was held up at the desk.'

Lisa watched as he settled in his seat,

dumping a bag beside him. What reason could there have been for his delay unless it was yet another telephone call? Narrowing her eyes, she looked at his bag wondering what was in it. Could it be his camera? No, that was in its usual place over his shoulder. So what would a man bring on a short afternoon trip? Suspiciously she eyed it until her thoughts were interrupted by Andy asking if they were ready to move off.

'Right, Andy,' she said brightly. 'Take it away.'

Positioning herself in the aisle between the two front seats she began to speak. 'This afternoon we'll be going through the valley of . . . '

The vehicle lurched and she put out her right hand to steady herself against the back of the seat. Her fingers made contact with a brown arm that she was sure hadn't been there a few minutes before.

'We're on the straight and narrow now,' Andy called. 'Sorry about that. It's a nasty swing away from the hotel.'

There was some murmuring and re-settling and the tension was broken. Keeping her eyes on the middle and back of the vehicle she continued with her little talk. Soon she'd almost forgotten Mark as she gave out a few leaflets, carefully putting Mark's on the vacant seat beside him to avoid touching him in any way.

As she straightened up she knew instinctively that he was silently laughing at her and she subsided into her own seat, wriggling across as near to the window as possible. But he didn't let her rest. After a few moments he leaned across and touched her arm.

'Can you tell me when we're going to stop?'

Her natural concern for her passengers was evident as she answered, 'Is anything wrong? You're not ill?'

'Oh, not at all. I missed my breakfast and am looking forward to sampling those famous Austrian cakes.'

His deep tones carried and several people behind him laughed.

How dare he talk about missing breakfast like that, as though it were some kind of joke? When that particular meal was being served they'd both been at the tiny stream. Obviously their shared joy of the morning had not meant anything special to him. Icily she turned towards him.

'You should make sure you have all your meals. After all, they're included in the price.'

That should bring him down to the same level as us all, she thought with satisfaction.

'In any case, there is a bar at the hotel where you can get a lunchtime snack. Most of us use that.'

Then before he could reply she rose to her feet.

'At least one of our party is anxious for some refreshments. We shall be stopping in about twenty minutes.'

Seeing everyone off when they stopped, she made sure they knew where and when to rejoin the party noting with annoyance that Mark was still seated. Finally he stepped down to her.

'Don't worry, I know all the details,' he said sarcastically. 'I've been listening to you telling everyone the same thing.'

She stepped back, giving him the opportunity to pass but he stayed in the same position and looked her up and down.

'How efficient you look in that uniform. By the way, I did have my lunch. I wouldn't want you to worry about me.'

Then he turned on his heel and strode away.

A stroll along the lakeside with Andy restored her good humour. They lingered at the edge of the water laughing at the antics of some children

'Fancy going to the top?' he asked.

She tilted back her head to where the cable cars were crossing on their way up and down the mountain.

'You go, Andy. I fancy just wandering around.'

'Fine with me,' he answered. 'We'll

have a gentle walk and then coffee and cake.'

'That sounds great. I'm just not in the mood for anything more strenuous.'

'I know what you mean. It takes a couple of days to unwind after the drive. I reckon Jane's enjoying her afternoon off.'

'Is it serious between you two?' she asked with the ease of a long-standing friendship.

'Yea, I reckon it probably is.'

'The great British understatement! I'm glad for you both,' she said and squeezed his arm affectionately.

'When everything is settled, you'll be one of the first to know.'

'I'll look forward to that.'

She planted a swift kiss on his cheek knowing that he would take it in the spirit in which she intended.

The rest of the afternoon and the journey back were uneventful but it was later at the end of the evening meal that she regretted her spontaneous gesture in kissing Andy.

Mark caught her up on the way to her room and as she put her key into the lock he leaned against the door, putting her in a difficult position. If she opened the door, it would be as good as inviting him in so she hesitated with the key half turned and took refuge in conversation.

'Did you have a pleasant afternoon?'

He didn't answer her question immediately so she continued.

'I noticed you enjoying the cake. I was at the back of the restaurant.'

'You were there with the driver?'

'What, oh, Andy. Yes, he's an old friend.

'Yes, I noticed you were very friendly. I rather thought he was with the other girl.'

His tone left her in no doubt as to what he meant.

'What do you mean? They're both friends of mine.'

'I watched you at the side of the lake and you seemed rather more than just friendly.'

'You watched me? What's the matter with you? You're always watching me.'

'Perhaps I find you a very good subject.'

His voice was now a maddening drawl, which was the last straw and her control cracked.

'Well, you may find it amusing but I'm sick of it. You were watching me on the ferry and then when I was driving. You were watching me this afternoon when I was with Andy. What are you, some sort of . . . '

She nearly said spy and quickly altered it to the first thing that came into her head.

'Some sort of Peeping Tom.'

Her mouth was dry and her fingers tightened on her key until the metal dug painfully into her soft skin.

'Come now,' he murmured, 'aren't we getting this all a bit out of proportion? I merely saw you with this other fellow. You kissed him and you must admit you were flirting on the journey with those other young lads.'

'Flirting!'

Her head snapped up with her dark eyes blazing in her hot face.

'How dare you say I was flirting? I was only being friendly.'

'You seem very good at just being friendly. You're friendly to everyone, particularly if they are male. Not very professional, is it?'

Her throat moved but she was quite unable to put into words her feelings of anger, despair and hurt. He was misunderstanding her quite deliberately. She had to get away from him but he was still leaning against her door and he was too big for her to push away. As her mind searched feverishly for a solution, her body took over. Before she could control it her foot lifted and came down on his toe.

'So sorry,' she said and turned the key fully and opened her door.

Locking it from the inside, she leaned against it while the rage left her.

Unprofessional, that was what he had

said! Quickly she reached for the notebook as she wondered if he was now trying to discredit her personally. And if he was, just what could she do?

5

On waking, the first thing Lisa saw was the notebook, on her bedside table. Whatever the contents of the book, she should not have let a situation develop where she physically attacked a paying client, if stamping on a man's foot could be classed as an attack. There were a good many ways to describe her behaviour and among them was childish and the word she most dreaded, unprofessional.

In the cold light of morning she was guilty on all charges.

She even wondered if she should apologise but knew there would be no sincerity in such an apology and indeed her whole being cringed at the idea. And why should she, she fumed, pushing her feet into her shoes. He had been rude and his insinuations were out of order. He'd as good as hinted that she spent her time on these tours picking up men, any men, even her best friend's man. No, Mark Treherne deserved all that he'd got. Then her mind swung again and she saw the funny side of the situation.

What a pity, she grinned, that she hadn't kicked him harder.

In the meantime there was today's programme and the sooner she got down to business the better. She'd looked forward to this morning. It was supposed to be the day she was going to enjoy most and now the episode with Mark had spoiled her happy anticipation. Salzburg was her favourite city. There was always something fresh with its beautiful squares, each one leading from another through a series of arches.

She decided to skip breakfast and hoping that today would be just as special, she finished dressing. Trim and neat in her uniform she carefully made up her face and tied back her hair loosely in a velvet ribbon.

Cautiously she opened her door and

peered out. Not a soul around — it was now or never. Feeling like a criminal she closed her door softly and almost tiptoed past the door of the adjoining room fearing that if he heard her, he might come out and continue the argument of the previous night. But all was well and feeling confident and much less uneasy she walked from the hotel into the bright, morning sunshine.

Andy was at the wheel for the outward journey and she was looking forward to a girl-to-girl chat with Jane. Perhaps talking things over would help clear her mind. She had one foot on the step when she caught Jane's smile and saw her pat the seat beside her. Good, she thought, Jane is obviously looking forward to sharing the journey with me. With her eyes on her friend's face, her other foot lifted and suddenly she was pulled off balance and literally fell into an inelegant heap on to the seat beside Mark.

The awful man had actually had the effrontery to pull her down beside him.

She opened her mouth, full of indignation, but just in time she saw another couple ready to enter and knew that she could not make a scene. The door slid shut and they began to move.

'You owe me,' he said softly.

'What do you mean?'

Changing tactics, she turned large eyes to him, hoping her expression bore just the right amount of puzzled innocence.

'You know exactly what I mean and don't try acting the little girl with me.'

'If you're talking about last night,' she replied, immediately on the attack, 'I'm actually waiting for your apology. I did not like your insinuations. Not,' she added, 'that my behaviour is anything to do with you.'

That should put him in his place.

'Don't get clever with me.'

Deciding to play it cool she laughed lightly.

'You owe me an apology for the quite unfounded accusation you made.'

Was it her imagination or did he now

look very slightly abashed? It was obviously her imagination as he wouldn't let the subject drop.

'They didn't look unfounded to me. In any case, I thought you were acting in an unprofessional manner, especially for the boss's daughter.'

Keeping the lid on her temper was becoming more difficult but she managed to look him in the eyes.

'Is that anything to do with you?'

He hesitated long enough for her to know that he was thinking of an answer and she dreaded hearing his reply but when it came it was quite non-committal.

'Your attitude affects us all.'

Expecting him now to admit that he had a vested interest, she was lost for words and shrugged and turned her head away. Perhaps Jane would realise what was happening and call her over to her seat, but Jane just grinned at her.

'So,' he said softly, 'I repeat, you owe me.'

'And what exactly do I owe you?' she

inquired sweetly.

'Your company for the day.'

'Rubbish,' she snapped but she was genuinely surprised. 'That's just not on. I'm driving back anyway and besides I . . . '

'No problem. I've checked and you're free until the return journey.'

His smug, satisfied look was the last straw.

'What a pity I only stood on one of your toes,' she hissed quietly. 'But still, there's always another time.'

'I don't think so. You did tell me there is a facility for writing complaints about the holiday.'

Surely he was teasing.

'Are you daring to threaten me?'

'Perhaps.'

It was no answer and she turned from him, staring straight ahead. Surely he wouldn't make a complaint. She admitted that the only possible way was to go along with him and be his companion for the day. She couldn't have her father upset by even the most trivial complaint, especially when it concerned his daughter. Even though her decision was made she couldn't resist glaring back at him.

'I didn't see you when I came out of the hotel,' she said.

'Were you hoping I wasn't coming today?'

He looked down at her.

'Yes, I can see you were.'

'How did I miss you sitting here in the front seat?'

'I must have ducked down to my camera bag. I had an adjustment to make which must have been as you were walking towards us.'

She'd lost that argument and wished she'd never started it. Closing her eyes she settled back in the seat, pretending sleep. He might have won her as an escort but she didn't have to speak to him.

Somewhere in the hours that followed she forgot that she was paying a debt and relaxed once again in his company. Together they roamed the

Mozart square in Salzburg, pausing at the fountain to study the statue of the maestro himself. The atmosphere was so evocative that strains of his music could almost be heard whispering in the air like a delicate breath of wind.

The city kept his memory alive at every twist and turn as though now it wanted to pay homage to this great musician who was buried in a paupers' grave. As they lingered past tiny shops, a particular piece of crystal caught her attention, a beautifully-fashioned paperweight with white fire shining from it's many facets.

'It's beautiful,' she breathed with her nose almost pressed against the window. 'It would be just right for our desk at home.'

But when she ventured in to enquire the price, it was way out of her league.

'You didn't buy it?' he asked as she joined him outside.

'Er, no. Far too expensive,' she mumbled and quickly changed the subject. 'Shall we find somewhere for coffee and a roll? I missed breakfast this morning.'

The coffee in the little bakery was thick and hot and they leaned against the small bar sipping its reviving warmth. Bringing her a second cup, Mark excused himself.

'Just want to grab a postcard, back in a moment.'

He was gone before she could reply. Anyway, she adored coffee and it was easy to drink another one.

'I've nearly finished,' she greeted him on his return. 'Did you get what you wanted?'

'Sure,' he said briefly, patting his jacket. 'Someone I mustn't forget.'

The shaft of jealousy that tore through her body surprised her with its intensity. The thought that was hidden at the back of her mind suddenly burst forth like a flower in the sunshine until her heart was bursting with the knowledge that she was in danger of falling in love with him. It was ridiculous, for she knew nothing about him. She didn't know why he was here or what he did for a living.

As they walked through the Mirabelle Gardens, he casually took her hand and when they stopped to admire the flowers she found he was looking at her. For a second she met his glance and was surprised at the tenderness which was mingled with desire. A group walked nearby, making them aware that they were not alone and his hand tightened as they strolled on.

The remainder of their time was just a background to the sensations that were building up. Now the chemistry between them bouncing from one to the other was almost tangible, so real that Lisa believed she could stretch out and touch it. At last the spell was broken as time, relentless in its pursuit, crept up, telling her the beautiful day was over.

'I have to be at the coach early.'

She glanced at her watch willing it to be wrong.

'OK, I'll come with you.'

'No, please, don't bother. You can have another half hour in the city.'

'I'll come with you,' he insisted and once again she noticed the firm quality of his voice.

Now, quite perversely, she was eager to get rid of him. The magic had gone, driven away by the trite words. She shook her head.

'People will think . . . '

'That we've spent the day together? Well, we have.'

'Yes, but . . . '

Her voice drifted away and she admitted she was getting absolutely nowhere.

'Do you honestly believe that with a whole coachload of passengers in Salzburg that no-one has seen us walking around together? And does it matter?'

'Of course not,' she said quickly but knew the evening meal would bring, at the least, an inquisition from Jane.

She was right, for as she started to spoon up her soup she sensed that the other girl was bursting with questions and resigned herself to what was to come. Jane leaned forward.

'You're spending a lot of time with this man you don't like,' she teased.

Infuriatingly Lisa blushed.

'It's nothing.'

'You were seen,' Jane announced triumphantly, 'hand in hand, in the gardens.'

Lisa blushed deeper than ever.

'But I didn't notice you there.'

Then she realised she was making it worse.

'I'm not surprised,' Jane gloated. 'Your eyes were for him only. We were quite surprised to see you both back, weren't we?'

She turned to Andy for confirmation, and he grinned. He was obviously content to leave all the questioning to Jane.

'All right, we spent the day together,' she said impishly. 'The way you're going on anyone would think it was the night. Anyway,' she added primly, 'things are not always as they appear.'

'Don't give us that, Lisa. We're your

friends, remember?'

She turned to Andy and then back to Lisa.

'We were going to travel together and have a good gossip. What happened to that idea?'

What on earth could she say?

'I . . . er . . . sort of tripped and fell into that seat this morning and it went from there.'

As Jane spluttered into her soup, Lisa remembered her motive in spending the time with Mark. Now her suspicions came flooding back, drowning her new-found love. How could she have allowed herself to become so vulnerable to his charms and be so taken in that she imagined herself falling in love with him?

Sitting through the rest of the meal, listening to her friends recounting their own day, she once again struggled to clear her mind. Her mind, however, refused to be cleared and interwoven with the threads of conversation around her were the remembered silken skeins of her shared hours with Mark. The happiness and contentment of being with him lay alongside her worries and doubts. The scales were finely and evenly balanced. It now needed just one small thing to tip them either way.

As she gained the safety of her room that night she felt hot as she was still in uniform owing to them being late returning. Deciding to stay in her room and have an early night, she peeled off her clothes and showered quickly. Fresh and cool in a clean nightdress she thrust her arms into her wrap and went on to the balcony.

The night was dark and still. It had been a beautiful and enchanted day whatever Mark's motives and she resolved to telephone her father tomorrow. Perhaps, without even mentioning Mark's name, she could find out more about the company that was believed to be taking them over. How she desperately hoped now that he would not be involved.

Her thoughts idled and she barely

heard the soft knock on her door. Jane, she thought, had come for some further questioning. Perhaps she thinks I'll tell her more if we're alone.

But it was not Jane. It was Mark. His expression was uncertain and in his hand he clasped a tissue-wrapped package.

'Mark?' she questioned, belting her wrap securely around her.

'May I come in for a moment?'

'Of course.'

He was in the room before she realised what had happened.

'I bought you this.'

He pushed the small package towards her without his usual confidence.

'I know you liked it.'

She guessed what it would be and as she pulled away the tissue paper, the beautiful crystal paperweight winked its fire at her. Caught in the overhead light, its rainbow colours changed and merged again and again.

'Oh, Mark. It's so beautiful. But how can I accept it?'

He frowned his annoyance.

'What do you mean? It's a very small thankyou for a lovely day.'

The wheels of her mind turned over even as she turned the crystal again to the light.

'You didn't have to buy it. I thought I owed you a debt. I thought . . . '

Her voice cracked and she was close to tears. What was even worse, she had no clear idea what she was saying.

'It was just an excuse.'

He took the crystal from her and placed it by her bed.

'Excuse?'

'That ridiculous threat was only an excuse to be with you. Didn't you realise?'

Tears of relief filled her eyes. He did care, even if it was just a little. He did care.

Tenderly he brushed her hair from her forehead and ran his mouth over her eyelids and her cheeks until he reached her mouth. As his lips brushed hers with feathery, light strokes the world began to spin. His arms went round her, pressing tightly until the whole length of her body was clasped hard against him. The kiss went on, gathering intensity until Lisa drew back and tried to push him away.

'That's enough Mark, I . . . '

As his arms fell to his sides there was a clatter as something hit the floor. Leaning down he picked it up.

'Nothing important,' he said. 'Just a notebook.'

She looked at the small book he held before her as though it was a snake. Even its dark cover looked sinister. It swayed before her eyes as though waiting to strike, rearing over her and bringing to the surface all her doubts and fears that were pushed into the background with Mark's kiss. Sick and trembling, she grabbed at the book, hugging it to her. He mustn't see it and know what she had written.

But what if her writings were true? She could barely cope with the thought. Worst still, what if his advances were just a ploy to lull her fears? She'd been stupid enough to let him know that she suspected his motive of going to Austria with them. Would this be a way of keeping her quiet?

'What's so special about that book?'

He laughed and reached for it.

'I wonder what is written in it.'

Lisa put it behind her back and clasped it firmly until her fingers were numb.

'Please, leave, Mark. You shouldn't be here. It's not professional. I can't behave like this.'

'Unprofessional? It's different when it's Andy and the young men at my table,' he snapped and his eyes were suddenly cold as he turned on his heel and left the room.

She picked up the book and remembered what she had written. All her suspicions were outlined in black and white on the pages. But where was that confidence now when her heart was searching for ways to betray her reason?

Who was Mark? Was he a genuine

tour passenger or, was he an industrial spy?

The beautiful crystal sat mocking her, sending its rays of colour across the room.

6

Rubbing her eyes, Lisa rolled over and came face to face with the crystal paperweight. The tiny object winked and blinked obviously revelling in the light as though it was wishing her good-morning.

Gently she took it into her hand and watched it sparkle and shine as she turned it in every direction. The shafts of light pierced through the cotton wool of her thoughts. Now she remembered. He'd come to her room and brought a present. The object that had brought him to her still lay on her palm. Abruptly she placed it back on to the table as though its very fire was burning her fingers.

She had to admit it was beautiful and a lovely gift. If only she was sure of his motives. Unthinkingly she'd admired the piece in Salzburg, never dreaming that he would buy it for her. Was it a payment? Had he bought her companionship yesterday or was the gift just that, a spontaneous gesture of friendship and perhaps the hope for something more?

As she stared at the crystal, she knew she was going to keep it. If nothing else, it would be a poignant memory of a love that might have been — and never will be, her mind told her sternly as her thoughts started to drift with a dreamlike quality where last night's scene played with a different ending. But she couldn't go on thinking of what might have been and the sooner she was out of bed and getting on with the day the better.

Her musing was interrupted with a soft tap at the door. Swinging her legs to the floor, she clutched her wrap as though it was a lifeline and struggled into it. Feeling her mouth go dry, she swallowed and pulled the wrap more closely around her body. It had to be Mark.

There was another knock. This time it was more impatient and, summoning all her dignity and courage, she straightened her shoulders and swinging open the door she leaned against it in relief. Spread right across Jane's round face was a wicked grin.

'I'm not disturbing anything, am I?'

'Of course not.'

'Sleep well?'

Her eyes were pure mischief.

'Fair.'

Lisa knew she was blushing and turned away quickly, but Jane missed nothing.

'I see.'

She drew the syllables out to an exaggerated length and they hung in the air full of implication. Closing the door, Lisa waved her friend to a chair and once again sat on the bed. As she looked for a way of changing the subject she heard Jane continue and knew she wouldn't give up.

'Last night I heard voices. I could have sworn they were coming from this room.'

'Really.'

As she spoke, Lisa suddenly saw the amusing side of the situation. Jane was dying of curiosity and after all she was her friend.

'It was probably the radio or the TV.'

'You wretch. You know what I mean. Was it him?'

'He brought me something, that's all.'

The last phrase hung on the air, full of meaning, and she blinked back the tears that were threatening to fall.

'Lisa, are you all right? Trust me to go ranting off without thinking.'

She got up and looked down, studied the large dark eyes smudged in the pale face of the girl on the bed.

'Do you want to talk about it?'

'No thanks, not yet.'

Then noticing the air of suppressed excitement, she forced some brightness into her voice.

'So what's the situation with you and Andy?'

'Well, we haven't announced it yet,

but we're engaged.'

'Oh, Jane.'

Getting up, she flung her arms around her friend.

'I'm so very pleased for you both. Is there going to be a big celebration? Perhaps we could organise something here. I'm sure everyone would be thrilled to have this happen during their holiday.'

'Oh, Lisa, it would be great.'

Jane looked quickly at her watch.

'I must go. It's all right for those of us who have the day off. Go back to bed. You look exhausted and don't forget my shoulder is a good size if you want to cry on it or even just talk.'

'I know, Jane, and thanks.'

She shut the door after the flying figure. It was her day off and what on earth was she going to do with herself? The thought struck her that this was not usually a problem. She was happy with her own company and enjoyed browsing around. So why was today different? Her breath left her in a long sigh. As usual the cause was Mark.

As she showered and dressed, she muttered and murmured, giving herself a good talking-to as though she were another person. Crazy, I'm going absolutely crazy! She grinned. After that, things didn't appear quite so black and standing before the mirror she knew she looked and, more importantly, felt good. Her maudlin mood had completely vanished.

A quiet stroll to the village revived her spirits further and seating herself outside a flower-decked restaurant she ordered coffee and cake. As she sipped the hot, thick liquid she remembered the tiny bakery in Salzburg where they had taken their morning refreshment. Her resolution not to think about him crumbled like the rich chocolate torte on her plate.

She hated to condemn anyone and normally gave them the benefit of the doubt but she was far too involved. It was useless to try and work things out and in order to cosset herself, she forgot the hastily-lost pounds of a few weeks ago. Her order of more coffee also included yet another sinful portion of cake.

Deciding to have a snack lunch alone, later, she bought fruit, cheese and a roll and sauntered slowly back to her room. Fishing a paperback novel from her case and with her picnic prepared she settled herself on the balcony, laying back in her chair. She must have dozed for a few minutes when a noise brought her floating back to consciousness. A deep, rich voice slid through her senses like treacle.

'We have to talk, Lisa.'

The sound was low and seductive.

'Yes,' she breathed, only half awake.

'We have to talk.'

There it was again but there was also a scrambling and scratching sound and the balcony floor dipped slightly. Like a drop of cold water on her warm skin, the noise shattered her dream. Shaking her head to clear her drowsiness, her eyes opened and focussed on Mark.

Quickly she whisked her skirt down and began to sit up.

'Sorry if I startled you.'

He touched her shoulder as though to soothe but his touch, far from soothing burned through the silk of her shirt. Her paperback hit the floor as she swung her feet down and with a hand that shook slightly, she pushed her hair from her hot forehead.

'Talk,' she croaked trying to recall his words and picking on the only phrase that she remembered. She gestured to the only other chair.

'Sit down.'

It was said as much for her benefit as for his. He was far too big to deal with standing.

'I'm sorry.'

Startled, her eyes widened and she opened her mouth but he stopped her from speaking.

'I know what you're thinking.'

'You do?' she gasped, wondering what on earth he was talking about.

'I know how it must have looked.

Believe me, I'm sorry.'

She was puzzled but her hand was happy to stay engulfed in his when he reached out and grasped it.

'It was unthinking of me and I know I gave you entirely the wrong idea. I didn't come to your room with the intention of seducing you.'

'You didn't?'

Her thoughts wouldn't come together and she was conscious of answering incoherently. What must he think?

'Believe me.'

He sounded so sincere that she could only believe him and trust that her heart was right in its judgment.

'You didn't want to love me?' her voice was just a whisper.

He ran a hand through his hair.

'Of course I want to love you,' he said more firmly.

'Why did you come?'

'To bring you a present,' he said simply. 'I knew you wanted the crystal and when I watched your face with your nose pressed against the shop window I wanted to be the one to buy it for you.'

She studied his eyes, almost sure she saw some tenderness but then he spoiled it.

'Anyway, you said it was too expensive for you to buy yourself.'

'Don't patronise me,' she snapped, shattering the mood. 'I haven't got your money and goodness only knows what you're doing here but I've got my pride.'

'Please.'

He put both hands on her arms and pulled her gently to her feet.

'I'm just a holidaymaker who wanted to buy a present for a rather special girl. What does it matter how much it cost? It's not important. I only wanted to give it to you.'

His quiet sincerity won the day. It was a lovely gift.

'Thank you and I shall treasure it always.'

It was as though she was playing a scene and could stand back and watch herself as she thanked him so charmingly.

'It was very thoughtful of you and I'm sorry I spoiled it.'

She even raised herself and touched his cheek with an impersonal kiss.

'Can we start again, no strings?'

'No hidden motives,' she said.

'No hidden motives,' he agreed. 'We'll just be two people who've met on holiday.'

For a while they were silent, both busy with their own thoughts then Mark spoke again.

'Will you spend the rest of the day with me?'

She nodded.

'Let's take a cable car to the top and look down on the world.'

They left the hotel together and hand in hand walked to the cable car station. Hands still clasped, they looked down on the village as they moved slowly upwards.

Breathtaking views opened out from every angle and when she tensed as they slid over the cable supports, his arm circled and held her closely. Stupidly she wanted to put her head on his shoulder but she successfully cooled her emotions. By unspoken agreement they kept the conversation away from business and discovered mutual interest in music and books.

Lisa was happy, truly happy and Mark seemed equally content. He was careful to keep his touch light and casual and even though there were few people, he made no attempt to hold or kiss her. Instinctively she knew he was trying to build their relationship. Perhaps this time there would be nothing to spoil it.

But she was wrong. When they returned to the hotel, Mark was called to Reception and still holding her hand, he pulled her with him to the desk.

'A message for you, sir,' the reception clerk said and picked up a piece of paper. 'Your assistant is arriving in Salzburg this evening and would like to be met.'

'Thanks,' Mark took the paper abstractedly. 'I thought it would be tomorrow.'

He looked down at Lisa.

'I was going to suggest we played truant and had dinner in the village but perhaps another night.'

'It doesn't matter.'

Once again her pride came to her rescue.

'I couldn't manage it anyway. I think there's going to be a little celebration in the bar tonight.'

'Really? That's fine then. It's all worked out rather well.'

She expected him to at least ask what the celebration was about but his mind was obviously already on more important things. The atmosphere was suddenly spoiled and their easy companionship faded away. Mark was now abrupt and like the man she had first met.

Quickly she reached her room and picked up the notebook. Whoever heard of someone sending for their assistant when they were supposed to be on holiday? He was up to something. She didn't know yet what it was but she would find out. Also he must be an executive of some value to a company. No ordinary manager would incur the cost of flying out an assistant.

Determinedly, she read through the pages and tried to evaluate the impression of the man she'd written about and compare it to the Mark of this afternoon. He was like two people in one body and one of them she didn't like or trust.

Appalled at her change of heart, she waited for half an hour and went swiftly and silently past his door and along to the telephones. Perhaps she could find out what he was up to once and for all. With shaking hands she dialled the code for the UK and soon heard her father's voice. Cutting short his questions as to how the tour was going, she interrupted him.

'Dad, I'm more interested in how everything is your end.'

He picked up the anxiety in her voice.

'Are you all right, love?'

'Yes, yes,' she said softly, blinking rapidly and trying not to sound impatient. 'It's you I want to know about. How's the take-over?'

'Going through nicely. They just want to check on a few more things. Should be through very shortly, love. Then all our worries will be over.'

'Yes, yes, that's great. Dad, listen carefully,' she said casually, not wanting to alarm him. 'Do you know the name of the managing director of this group?'

'Just the accountant, nice young man, as you know. He was asking after you just the other day, Lisa. I think you made a hit with him.'

'Dad, can't stop long but could you find the name of the head man? Please, Dad, it's important.'

His voice sharpened.

'What's wrong, love? Are you sure you're all right?'

'Yes, yes, nothing to worry about. It's just that this name cropped up and I wondered . . . '

'What was the name?'

'Treherne, Mark Treherne.'

'No,' he said slowly, obviously thinking hard. 'I'm not aware of anyone of that name.'

Relief flooded over her. All her suspicions were unfounded. Now she could accept Mark as he was and their relationship would be able to develop. She leaned against the wall. He'd certainly been keen to put himself right in her eyes today.

'Wait a moment,' her father spoke again. 'Those initials are familiar. I think I may have seen M.T. somewhere but why . . . '

Her lovely cocoon of warmth and happiness crumbled. She didn't want to worry her father but she had to know. Neither did she want him asking too many questions at this stage.

'Must dash, Dad. This is costing me a fortune. I'll ring in a couple of days, but please try and find out for me. 'Bye, Dad.'

Slowly she replaced the receiver, hoping that her father was wrong about the initials but with an awful sinking feeling she guessed that he was right. If Mark was indeed the managing director, what on earth was he doing with her? Her father thought that all their worries would soon be over but if she was right and Mark was involved in the take-over, they could just be beginning. There could be only one reason that he was here and that was to watch how the tour was run. Perhaps he was even now speaking into a tape recorder reporting on her, Jane and Andy.

She remembered the papers on his seat, how he always appeared to be studying them when they went on trips. She'd even wondered if he was a travel writer but she was sure now that he wasn't describing the scenery.

Her father had been assured that he would be kept on to run Corane Tours even when he no longer owned it.

Desperately she tried to remember more details of what had happened before she'd left home. Was it part of a contract? Had he got it in writing or was it just a verbal agreement?

Her father must be kept on. He'd spent his life running the business and now his only way out was to sell to a larger company. It was so unfair.

If Mark was involved, would their jobs be secure? Well, maybe some of them, she considered, but probably not herself. He still hated women drivers. She was positive that he hadn't changed his mind about that subject. She would have to cope with finding something else but she would hate to think that any disagreement she might have with Mark would influence her father's position.

Even though she obviously appealed to him physically, would it be enough to keep her father secure? The appalling thought sprang to the front of her mind that if she put a foot wrong on this holiday, he might even get rid of them both and what about Jane and Andy?

If only she could spend time thinking it through perhaps she might be able to come up with a solution, but tonight she must think of her friends. Jane and Andy would be celebrating their engagement. Knowing Jane, she guessed that everyone in the hotel would know by this evening. Her own problems must be shelved while she mingled with the others and tried to look happy and relaxed. She must smile and say the right things, knowing that Mark was meeting his assistant and that could only mean there were business problems brewing.

If only she could find out what they were.

7

Putting on her uniform the next day, Lisa recalled what a happy evening it had turned out to be. Her friends were so delighted with each other that it was a joy to see them. As she'd kissed Andy to congratulate him, she'd felt a faint pang of jealousy, a fleeting moment when she'd wished there was someone in her own life.

Applying a second coat of mascara now, she hoped no-one would notice the smudges under her eyes. Sleep had eluded her yet again while she tossed and turned, ever conscious of Mark on the other side of the wall and wondering if he was aware of her restlessness. She couldn't hear any sounds of life from his room and guessed he was recovering from sampling the local brew with his assistant. Just the sort of thing to expect from a couple of men.

Hurriedly she finished her make-up, glancing at her watch as she left the room. Quickening her pace she knew she'd better hurry to breakfast as the lake tour was due to leave at half past nine and when she was driving she needed a good meal to keep up her energy level.

Edging in beside her friends, she noticed they looked worse than she felt! Jane was trim in her waistcoat and skirt but for once her normally round, bright face was tired and hollowed and she just smiled her greeting as though it was too much trouble to speak. Andy was in shorts.

'Thank goodness I've got some time off,' he said. 'The local beer must be stronger than I thought.'

'More likely the liqueur you were drinking at the end,' Jane said with a grin. 'But at least you can have an easy morning.'

Suddenly Jane's attention left them.

'Wow, take a look at that. I haven't seen her before.'

The other two heads swivelled in unison. Andy let out a low, appreciative whistle. The woman was tall and slender but curved in just the right places. Her blonde hair was pulled back into a long plait which left her face unframed in all its classical beauty. She wore the briefest of shorts, a clinging top and walked with the air of one who knows she is being watched.

'Who is she? No-one has the right to look like that first thing in the morning.'

Looking at the blonde woman, Lisa felt more drained than ever.

'Look where she's heading.'

Jane grabbed her arm and her fingers dug hard into Lisa's flesh.

She should have known. The woman was making for a small table for two at which sat Mark. As though in a dream, Lisa watched him get up and hold a chair out for her. Vaguely she could hear the other two still speaking but her whole attention was riveted on the far table. It was no coincidence that the girl had been put with Mark as the two heads met across the small space. They were very much two people who had a lot to talk about.

Surely this vision couldn't be his assistant! It wouldn't be fair. No-one should have such a generous amount of both brains and beauty. She must be mistaken but she knew that she was not. Her female intuition told her very positively that this was the person he'd rushed off to meet last night.

No wonder he'd dumped me, Lisa thought. After all, dinner in the village with an ordinary employee of the company wouldn't bare comparison with an evening with this cool, slender girl.

'Lisa,' Jane said as she tried to attract her attention. 'Everything OK?'

Lisa couldn't answer. Suddenly she'd had enough and, scraping back her chair and mumbling about bringing round the coach, she left the dining-room. Something to do, that's what she needed. Something to take her whole attention and occupy her mind while the implication of the two at the other table was shelved.

Unlocking the coach she swung herself up and settled in the seat. Now she was more than glad that it wasn't a day of leisure. She needed to be fully occupied. Automatically, her hands went to the controls. There was an awful and ominous silence. The vehicle didn't start. Desperately she repeated the sequence. Again and again her fingers pulled and pushed while she mentally checked she was doing all the right things as though she doubted her own sanity, but it wouldn't start.

Banging her head on the steering-wheel, she felt the coldness of defeat flow through her bones. What was she going to do? It just wouldn't start. A breakdown was something she dreaded. No matter how many times they were told it almost never happened she had nevertheless dreaded a time when it might.

She must get Andy out here quickly

before anyone realised that anything was wrong. Jumping down, she jarred her ankle and panicked that she'd sprained it but it was part of her imagination and she almost ran back to the hotel. Rapidly, she walked over to Jane and Andy. Hoping no-one would notice her agitation, she bent down and whispered to Andy while watching the alarm that registered on his face.

'Electrics,' he muttered. 'Go back and act as though nothing is wrong. I'll be with you in a moment.'

She didn't glance in the direction of Mark but somehow knew he was picking up vibrations that something was wrong. From the corner of her eye she saw him leave his seat and as she tried not to run, she knew she was being followed.

'Anything the matter?' he inquired as he caught up.

'Of course not,' she answered sharply. 'What could there be?'

'Just that you appear to be troubled.'

'I'm surprised you noticed,' she

snapped and then could have bitten off her tongue. 'I mean,' she tried to qualify her statement, 'you must be busy with your . . . er . . . assistant.'

'Oh, yes,' he said casually, 'you noticed Chris at breakfast.'

At least her sarcasm had been lost and for that she was grateful. The last thing she wished was for him to think that she was jealous. He stood back eyeing the coach speculatively.

'How long do you keep your transport?'

'All depends,' she said airily, knowing that it had been some considerable time since anything new had been bought.

'Poor marketing,' he said almost to himself.

He then had the audacity to circle around slowly as though he was mentally making notes on any short-falls.

'Doesn't do a company's image any good to run an old fleet.'

She was so angry that phrases battled for space inside her head, nasty little phrases to put this arrogant man in his place but so fierce was the battle that her throat was paralysed. He watched with a slight lift of an eyebrow as though he knew the struggle taking place inside her head.

At last she managed to force out, 'You patronising, horrible, man! Do you know how much these things cost? Anyway, who are you? Don't tell me you're just here for the ride, because I don't believe it. I can't see anyone else taking this attitude.'

'Hey, steady. I only meant to make a few points.'

He placed a hand on each side of her upper arms as though to soothe a spoiled child. Pushing his hands away, she fixed him with eyes that were glinting with daggers that threatened at any moment to find their mark on him. Not wanting to hear anymore she interrupted rudely.

'I don't need you to point out anything. There's absolutely nothing wrong, nothing.'

'Really?' he drawled. 'Then why is Andy making his way here? I thought it was his day off.'

Andy was moving nearer with every moment and as though in a nightmare she watched helplessly while he walked straight to Mark. Obviously he assumed the older man knew about the problem and was trying to help.

'It's all right. I can guess the problem. Those blasted electrics again. It'll have to go into a garage when we're back, but I think I can fix it.'

She didn't dare look at Mark. She may have lied but it was in a good cause. Mark was forgotten as yet another complication occurred as people began to flock from the hotel carrying bags and cameras, ready for the morning excursion. Searching desperately for a way to head them off she ran up to the first group.

'Spot of bother,' she said and smiled with what she hoped was complete naturalness. 'Won't be more than half an hour so if you like to come back with me I'll organise some free coffee while you're waiting.'

Five hectic minutes later she dashed back. Mark was forgotten as she dealt with the immediate problem.

'I've told them half an hour,' she called to Andy. 'What do you think?'

'It'll be done by then,' he answered with his attention focused fully on the job in hand.

'You've got a good man there. Not everyone would be so willing to deal with this on their free day,' Mark stated.

It was then she knew for certain in her own mind that everything she suspected about Mark must be true. How did he always know their rotas? No-one but the staff knew who was on duty and his few words about Andy were those of a prospective employer weighing up the staff.

'Don't look so dejected,' he went on. 'You dealt with the situation very well.'

She smiled slightly, knowing that however much she imagined she hated him, she was stupidly pleased at his praise.

'Doesn't do to let people know anything about breakdowns.'

He was still speaking.

'It takes away their confidence and puts them off travelling with you again. You can't afford to lose any business, can you?'

'Are you put off?' she asked coldly, knowing she was experiencing yet another change of mood.

'Me?'

He seemed surprised.

'Yes, you,' she insisted. 'You're an ordinary tourist, aren't you? At least that's what you keep telling me. And of course, it's quite normal for you to send for your assistant, isn't it? It's done all the time on holidays!'

'It's all right now,' Andy said. 'Go and call your passengers.'

Looking at her, he frowned as though he could read her thoughts.

'No, don't you worry. I'll tell Jane to bring them out. Try to relax, Lisa.'

'Thanks,' she said gratefully. 'I'll be sure to tell Dad how helpful you've been.'

Suddenly drained of energy, she even allowed Mark to help her up the coach steps. Mentally she crossed her fingers that no-one would be too difficult. Then a spontaneous cheer reached her ears and everyone was laughing and talking as they clambered in. Sara and Jo gave her the thumbs-up sign and she realised she had become so involved with Mark that she had almost forgotten the existence of the other holidaymakers.

Mark's shoulders filled the doorway and he bent over her and once again all else was forgotten.

'You'll be all right now,' he said softly, then added, 'and don't take everything so much to heart. You've only lost half an hour and they've all taken it well.'

Ruefully she remembered the times when she'd wished his irritating presence was left behind and now when she quite desperately wanted him with her, he was giving this morning's excursion a miss.

Jane, however, appreciated the absence of Mark.

'Hey,' she said when they stopped for coffee, 'at least we can have some time together today.'

'I'm sorry, Jane. I know I've neglected you but things haven't been easy and in any case you've got Andy now.'

'Well, Andy isn't here today.'

Jane followed her from the vehicle, still talking.

'There's just you and me and I want to hear all the latest news about that man.'

'Man?' Lisa repeated innocently. 'What man?'

'Hey, what's the idea?'

Jane's eyes were round and bright with interest as they faced each other across two steaming coffees.

'I don't mind being abandoned in favour of a guy but a guy you profess not to like, well that's another matter.'

'But I don't like him,' Lisa hissed through clenched teeth.

'Well, you could have fooled me. That day when you weren't driving, you were going to sit and chat with me and what happens? One foot on the step and you were practically on his lap.'

Suddenly it was too much and Lisa's eyes filled with tears.

'I can't explain. I would tell you if I could. I really don't like him, at least I think I don't and then sometimes I like him too much. The problem is I don't trust him. He's not one of the crowd and I suspect he's got a motive for being here.'

'I was only teasing you.'

Jane's face was concerned.

'Forget I asked.'

After that, the subject was closed but Lisa couldn't put Mark from her thoughts. Then as though it were planned, the first thing she saw as she passed the main lounge on their return were the blonde and dark heads close together.

Trying to put them from her mind, she dressed for the planned wine-tasting and folk evening in a peasant-style dress in black and rose. The outfit gave her a gipsyish air and she twirled in front of the mirror, admiring the effect. When she reached the bar, she found that long tables were set up and catching sight of Sara and Jo, she joined them. Laughing with the girls, her mood lifted as they all sipped and gave their opinions on the wine. After the tasting, accordion music started quietly and then became more boisterous. Fingers flew over keyboards and the men from the village stamped and strutted in national costume.

A slight touch on her shoulder made her swing round to see Mark. He'd just bent his head to say something in her ear when she saw Chris's face over his shoulder.

'Thank goodness I caught you,' Lisa heard her say. 'I need you to look at some papers in my room.'

Lisa thought his lips formed the word

later to her as he turned away from her. Her eyes followed them from the room as she wondered just how long the business meeting would take. But he didn't come back to join them.

She was just on the edge of sleep when she thought she heard a knock on her door, but the events of the day proved too much for her and she turned and fell into a deep sleep.

8

Luxuriously stretching in the aftermath of sleep, a faint alarm bell rang in her mind. Reluctantly she began to wake remembering that for some reason she didn't want to get up today. There was something she had to face so she tried to keep her thoughts blanketed with slumber. Two things surfaced, however. One was the glamorous woman with Mark and the second that she might hear from her father.

The events from the previous day had left her fragile and not at all like her normal energetic self. But eventually she swung her legs from the bed and quickly showered and dressed. Satisfied with her appearance and ready to face the day, she turned the key in the lock to open her door, but when she opened it, Mark was standing outside.

'I was listening through the wall to

your movements,' he said shamelessly. 'You didn't answer your door last night.'

The comment was said so casually and his face was so bland that Lisa couldn't believe what she was hearing.

'Did you expect me to?' she said with a cutting edge. 'I don't care to be part of your collection of women.'

Strangely he appeared genuinely puzzled.

'What do you mean?'

Could he really be that innocent? No, he obviously thought she was so naïve that she didn't know what was going on.

'Your . . . er . . . assistant.'

The hesitation was slight but found its home as his mouth tightened.

'So?'

'You can't deny you were in her room.'

'Why should I? What is all this about?'

'It's better I keep away from you,' she muttered.

'Why didn't you open your door?'

'Because I was tired, of course. You know the problem I had with the coach in the morning.'

Immediately, she wanted to withdraw what she'd said but it was too late. Before he could answer she frantically changed the subject.

'And then, of course, there's your so-called assistant. Who calls for an assistant in the middle of a holiday? Who goes over papers at night in her room? Do you think I'm stupid?'

They stared at each other as though each deciding how to go for the kill. Then from around the corner a woman appeared in a white apron. Fresh towels were draped across one arm while she trundled a cleaner in front of her with the other.

'All right to do your room, sir?' she said to Mark and broke the spell.

Without waiting for his reply, Lisa took her opportunity and fled. By subtle manoeuvring she managed to avoid him for the rest of that day and part of the next.

Throwing herself into all the activities, she surrounded herself with people. It was quiet now with most of the excursions finished and everyone was wandering around enjoying the local walks and buying last-minute gifts and souvenirs to take home.

Lisa tagged along with Jo and Sara and the young men. In normal circumstances she would have been happy to spend time with them but now the men appeared immature and boyish and she knew she was comparing them with Mark.

With great energy she joined in anything that was going on and was so convincing that Jane and Andy who normally kept an eye on her, left her alone and devoted their time to each other. She was playing her part so brilliantly that she appeared to fool everyone. She was certain she wouldn't hear any more from Mark.

She caught sight of him at meal times when he appeared frequently with

Chris and they were always deep in conversation. They had to be an item and she was so resigned to the fact that when she answered the telephone one day in her room and heard his voice, the receiver dangled from her weakened hand.

'Lisa,' he said abruptly, 'why do I have the feeling you're avoiding me?'

Gathering her wits she said stiltedly, 'Perhaps because I am.'

'Would you have dinner with me tonight in the village? We need to get away and talk.'

'There's nothing to say,' she replied rudely.

'I disagree. We have a lot to talk about. There are things to be cleared up between us.'

'Look, I hate to waste your time. I also think it's ill-mannered to put the phone down while someone is speaking but there is no reason for us to have dinner that I can think of and, believe me, I will hang up if you don't give me a good reason to go out with you.'

That should finish his argument and she was ready to replace the receiver when after a brief hesitation she heard.

'Don't hang up. I'm asking you to dinner because we need to talk but mainly because I want to be with you.'

Her resolutions of the past two days melted, he sounded so sincere.

'Well,' she hesitated.

'Good. There's a superb place in the village. I had a meal there the other night.'

Suddenly her mind snapped into gear. That meant he had taken Chris there for dinner one night. Jealousy caused her hands to clench around the telephone.

'No,' she hissed rapidly. 'No, I don't want to go with you.'

'What?' The gentleness had gone from his voice. 'Am I allowed to ask why?'

'You may ask,' she drawled, 'but I won't tell you.'

'If you change your mind, ring me.'

The receiver crashed down at his end

and she slowly replaced her own. How dare he take her to a place where he'd taken the other girl! What gave him the right to think he could go from one girl to another?

Deciding she needed a good walk to clear her head, she searched for some flat shoes and hurriedly left her room. The slope behind the hotel was a steep climb and as she staggered up, it seemed her hatred of Mark grew with every step. Finally her energy was completely taken up with the climb and her anger faded with the physical exertion of staying on the track.

Feeling weary, she reached a small clearing at the side of the path and flung herself on to a wooden bench. Idly she sat listening to the faint gurgle of a nearby stream and wondered how she could feel so warm and still look up to the cold snow caps of the distant mountains.

A stone rolled to her feet and she looked up to see what had disturbed it. She saw Chris climbing down to her, positively the last person she wanted to see. Giving her a rather stilted half smile, Lisa assumed the other girl would pass by. She almost panicked when she flopped gracefully down on to the bench beside her and said softly, 'Beautiful day.'

Lisa nodded, not wanting to be involved in a conversation.

'Just making the most of my last day,' she went on, appearing not to notice the lack of warmth in Lisa. 'Now all the work's done I can go home, thank goodness.'

'You've finished?'

In spite of herself Lisa found she was responding.

'Yes, I've left my husband long enough. He hates it when I'm away.'

It took several seconds for this information to sink in. It was so at odds with the picture in her mind.

'Your husband?'

Lisa found her tongue and looked quickly at the girl's left hand.

Seeing her glance, she laughed.

'I don't always wear a ring. Some-times in business it's better to appear more liberated but I am definitely married.'

'I thought that you and Mark . . .'

Lisa's tongue was running away with her again.

'Sorry, it's none of my business,' she finished abruptly.

'Oh, Mark. Yes, he's a sweetie but not my type. He's too high-powered. I prefer a quieter type of man.'

The picture crumbled even further.

'But you seem pretty high-powered yourself.'

The girl looked amused.

'Yes,' she said thoughtfully, 'I suppose I am. It's always said that opposites attract.'

She got up.

'I'm being collected in an hour for the airport so I'd better get going.'

When the long, tanned legs had disappeared, Lisa realised she hadn't even answered Chris's casual goodbye. Sitting there, no longer noticing the heat of the sun on her shoulders, all she could think was that Mark had told the truth that there was nothing between him and Chris. He had said phone if she changed her mind about dining with him and she was going to throw her pride to the wind tell him she had definitely changed her mind.

Dashing to her room she dialled his number knowing that he was probably out enjoying the sun but he answered immediately. It was far easier than she'd expected.

All he said was, 'Would you wear that peasant dress you wore the other night?'

Weak with relief, she lay back on the bed and for the first time in days allowed herself to relax.

Never before had she taken so long and so much trouble to prepare for a date. With her make-up perfect and her hair freshly washed and shining she knew that she looked her best. The sun had given her skin an extra glow and streaked her hair with pale strands.

The restaurant lived up to Mark's description. It was absolutely charming. The conversation flowed as easily as the wine.

She was so used to the continual sniping and arguments between them that when the evening didn't develop into the usual battleground it seemed that they were two different people. In her mind, she could see them together looking as she always wanted them to look — two people enjoying the company of each other.

For a time the atmosphere was light and then a change occurred and the air became heavy with promises waiting to be spoken. They both refused dessert but sipped at the thick, Austrian coffee. Suddenly she panicked and ordered another cup, anxious to stay in the safety of the restaurant but although he sat patiently while she slowly drank she could prolong the meal no longer and they left.

Outside, the night was beautiful and with arms around each other, they turned to start the climb up the hill back to the hotel. At one point they stopped and looked back and were even more aware of the velvet darkness that surrounded them. He hesitated with her outside her room.

Impulsively she said, 'I'm sorry for the things I said about you and Chris. I had no right to comment on anything you do.'

'But you do have the right, Lisa. When are you going to realise that? You just have to learn to trust me.'

'Trust you?' she echoed as his arms went round her, then added silently, Oh, Mark, if only I could.

9

Lisa awoke slowly and lay reliving their evening together. From the moment when they left the hotel until the minute they returned, every word and touch was etched on her memory.

Twisting her head, she again saw the crystal paperweight sparkle in the clear light and, screwing up her eyes, she tried to read the message it was giving out. Impossible to decide if it sparkled with amusement or did the fire shooting from its shiny surface mean passion? Picking it up, she gazed at it long and hard, frowning and questioning as if it knew her fate.

However, it didn't warn her the telephone was about to ring and that it would be his warm, seductive voice wishing her good morning.

'You slept well?' he queried.

'Absolutely soundly. It was obviously the wine.'

'I hoped it was my company,' he said softly.

'Maybe that as well,' she admitted.

'Unfortunately, I've one or two things to do today which should only take a couple of hours.'

'Oh.'

She hoped he wasn't aware of her disappointment down the line. She mustn't let him know how much she wanted to be with him. Why didn't he want to see her earlier?

'So if we meet, say about half past eleven and take it from there, is that all right with you?'

'Perfectly,' she answered brightly and then just in case he thought she was waiting around for him she added, 'I've things to do myself, telephone calls to make and notes to write.'

'Telephone calls?'

His voice sharpened and there was a silence as though he was waiting for her to enlarge her statement and perhaps give him some details.

'Yes, so I'll see you later.'

She hung up, wondering why he reacted to her remarks about telephone calls. Then she dismissed it as unimportant or probably her over-sensitive imagination.

I might call Dad anyway, she mused and then realised that her father hadn't called her back with any information about the elusive initials. So there was probably nothing to report and her heart lifted. In a way, although not one word of love had passed between them, she knew that secretly she'd made a mental commitment to Mark and hoped nothing would happen to spoil it.

Checking the time, she wondered how she was going to fill the hours until she saw him. Pulling on her jeans and matching blue shirt, she went down to breakfast. She was late and the area was already full of people. Everyone was there but Mark. Sitting down and greeting Andy, she registered that Jane was also missing.

'She's gone back to her room for something she's forgotten,' Andy said.

Then Jane was rushing across towards them.

'What's your friend, Mark, up to?' she said to Lisa without even bothering about saying good morning, but pulling out her chair. 'There's quite a lot going on at reception. He's telephoning in the booth and at the same time being paged because there's another call coming through for him on a different line. It was quite high-powered stuff. I lingered to see if I could find out what was going on.'

'And did you?'

Lisa had trouble with words that suddenly stuck in her dry mouth.

'Not really, except that he was scribbling away like crazy on a large clipboard and you could tell from his face that it wasn't a casual chat with a friend. This was business and big business all the way.'

She looked at Lisa, obviously expecting some response and noticed her stricken expression.

'You OK this morning, Lisa?' she asked.

'Yes, of course. Actually, Mark told me he was expecting some telephone calls.'

She tried to appear casual.

'Oh, you've seen him then this morning?'

'Not exactly. I just know he had calls to make.'

Jane frowned as though trying to judge her friend's mood.

'I think something is going on and only wondered if you ought to know.'

'Do you think it's something to do with us?'

'I couldn't tell but I know something pretty important is happening.'

Jane was obviously considering what she should say.

'From the bits and pieces you've told me and the fact that his so-called assistant was here, I'd say something is definitely going on.'

Looking at her food, Lisa knew that she couldn't eat another thing.

'Maybe I'll skip breakfast.'

She left her friends, who looked after her with worried eyes and then looked at each other.

'Leave her to work it out,' Andy said softly. 'Don't interfere, Jane. There's nothing we can do.'

Lisa went to her room first and, sitting on the bed, tried to work through what Jane had told her. It could mean everything or it could mean nothing. Hopefully it was a bad attack of imagination. Jane was pretty down-to-earth, although being recently engaged she could be forgiven a few flights of fancy. It would be better to ignore the whole thing and put it out of her mind.

However, it refused to be put from her mind and reluctantly facing the fact that there was no other way to find out, she made her way to reception. Her legs were leaden as though trying to move through a bad dream.

Oh, please, she whispered continually, please let him not be involved in anything that affects Dad, especially after last night.

At the end of the corridor she hesitated and then, squaring her shoulders, marched on. All was quiet in the hotel entrance. There was just one clerk at the desk. The telephone wasn't ringing and there was no-one in the booth. Maybe Jane had dreamed it all but she was uneasy and there was only one way to find out and that was to ring her father.

It was difficult to get through. The lines were engaged and after trying continuously, she accepted the offer of the desk clerk to call her when it was clear and went to the bar for a coffee. Her hands were cold and she warmed them around the cup, hoping everything would be all right.

The call took a long time. She didn't say very much to her father but listened a great deal and when she slowly replaced the receiver, her hand was shaking badly. For days she'd thought and talked about them being taken over but at the back of her mind had hoped something would happen to prevent it. But there was to be no reprieve. Her father had signed the papers making Corane Tours over to Treherne Holdings, to Mark Treherne! Blinking rapidly, she was unable to stop the slow flow of tears that spilled down her cheeks.

Her father had sounded depressed and so old that she was quite alarmed. In reply to her question of his own future, he'd answered shortly that he didn't yet know and had been so dispirited that she'd wanted to dash home. Leaning against the cubicle, her legs shook. Even knowing that Jane, Andy and herself were assured positions could not compensate for the fact that Mark was now her boss.

Surely it was just a formality and he'd find a way to be rid of her. To him she'd be no more than an irritating fly upon the wall. He would flick her away without the blink of an eyelid. But what if he let her stay? She couldn't work for him, she just couldn't. If she didn't stay, if she gathered up her pride and walked out now, what then? The idea had great appeal, for the journey back could only be completed with two drivers.

She smiled grimly as she thought of the cost and inconvenience of flying someone out to take her place. Would the satisfaction of getting the better of him be worth it? She could go home, sure that her father would understand but she'd be dependent on him until she found another job.

She needed to be in the fresh air and was in the village and beside the little stream before she realised how far she'd walked. Had Mark played a part all this time? If so, he was a good actor, for he'd lulled her suspicions eventually and she thought she was starting to fall in love. Could she really have mis-judged a man so very much?

'Your father rang again,' she was told

at reception on her return.

'Thanks. I'll get back to him.'

'He left a message saying he was out for the rest of the day and would call again tomorrow.'

'Thanks,' she called over her shoulder as she made for her room.

A note had been pushed under her door.

Darling Lisa, it read, *where were you? Meet me in the bar any time. M.T.*

It was those meaningful initials that made her so mad. Picking up a pen she wrote **JUDAS** in big letters across the top, refolded it and pushed it under his door. Certain that he wasn't in his room, she opened her doors to the balcony and sank into the chair. There was so much she should have asked her father when they'd spoken but the shock had driven everything from her mind. Sitting with her eyes shut, she didn't see or even hear Mark come out of his room.

'Is this some kind of a joke?'

Her eyes opened abruptly and she saw him leaning over the rail with the note in his hand. Springing up, she stood behind her chair as though for protection.

'You know it isn't a joke,' she said furiously, her hands clenching and unclenching at her sides. 'What have you done to my father?'

With one vault, he was over the rail and standing beside her.

'Oh, I see that you know.'

He looked worried and smiled thinly.

'I was going to tell you this morning. I was going to explain everything.'

'There's nothing to explain. It's all done, isn't it? To think I believed you when you said you wanted to be with me. What an absolute fool I've been. It wasn't me you were interested in, was it?'

He reached for her shoulders as though he wanted to stop her talking but she pushed him away.

'All these days you've appeared wherever I've been. I couldn't drink a cup of coffee without you being at the other side of the table.'

'It wasn't like that. I know it seemed like that but . . . '

'Why couldn't I see that all the time you were using me?'

Her eyes closed as though she couldn't cope with looking at him.

'If you'd be quiet a minute you'd know how wrong you are. I admit I've been taking notes and watching points. If I'm going to have the company, I want to know how it's been run.'

Her eyes snapped open, glittering with hatred but he continued.

'I believe in finding out for myself first hand.'

'You're disgusting and underhanded and . . . '

'I had no need to spend so much time with you,' he interrupted and his voice became softer. 'I did that for myself, not the company.'

'Rubbish,' she spat out. 'You are the company.'

'I'm answerable to my shareholders,'

he said stiffly. 'I had to see for myself why you've been losing so much money.'

'You think we're inefficient?'

'No, not at all.'

'Then what? What's the point of all the cloak-and-dagger stuff?'

'Please, Lisa, listen to me.'

'So what is your opinion of our humble operation?'

'You should put up your prices. You're running on a shoestring.'

'We tried not to put up prices this year.'

'Not only this year but last year as well. It's a simple case of economics. You're giving people too much for their money.'

'But Dad said . . . '

'I know.'

He managed to take her resisting body into his arms.

'I'm sorry, but your father was wrong. He should have done his sums better and when I take over, the prices will go up. They'll have to or there'll be no more Corane Tours.'

All she heard was, no more Corane Tours. Momentarily her head drooped but just as quickly her temper rose.

'How could you throw a man of Dad's age out of a job?'

She pushed herself away from him so violently that she came up against the rail of the balcony.

'He won't be out of a job.'

'That's not what he thinks. It's his world, 'specially now that he hasn't got Mum.'

'I've personally safeguarded his position. Of course, there will be changes.'

'Yes, one big change and that is it won't be Dad's company any more and he won't be running it.'

'You stupid woman, why won't you listen?'

He was fast losing his temper and they glared at each other.

'If you want to know why I'll put up the prices it's because you need new equipment, better coaches, and videos that work, vehicles that don't break down. Do you want me to go on?'

How could he throw everything in her face like this?

'So that's what you've been watching for, all the faults, all the little things that don't really matter!'

Her shoulders slumped and she knew she was beaten.

'We've not had people complain.'

'Then you've been lucky.'

'And you've been shifty.'

She drew herself up to her full height and still looked up at him.

'Go away from me. I hate you and everything you stand for. I hope everyone refuses to work for you. I certainly will,' she added childishly.

She swept into her room and shut the balcony doors. He stood perfectly still with no expression on his face, which infuriated her even more. She slid the lock home and then as though that wasn't enough, reached up and drew the curtains across, shutting out his image from her eyes but not from her mind.

10

Triumphantly she threw herself on the bed, revelling in the knowledge that for once she'd got the better of him. At last she had the upper hand but seconds later she was worried again. Having convinced herself she'd gained points in their relationship she suddenly wondered what she was going to do now.

She hadn't given a single thought to how Mark would react. Surely he would go away quietly. He couldn't make a scene, for the adverse publicity to himself and his company would be terrible. Her heart hammered as she imagined him banging and rattling the door and calling out but he was quiet. But perhaps he wouldn't be quiet for long and the idea of someone the other side of her curtained window was frightening. Was he still there? How she longed to peep out but to be caught in

such a childlike act would be unthink-
able.

Even with the drawn curtains shutting him out she was uneasy. Despite
the fact that it was her room and he had
no right to be on her balcony, she was
unable to throw off her anxiety.
Nervously she glanced around, pacing
the small area, knowing she must get
out and go where he couldn't find her
for the next few hours.

Without knowing how she'd arrived
outside her own room she found that
she was quite literally hammering on
Jane's door. She practically fell into the
room as the door opened.

'Lisa!'

Jane's eyes were round with concern.

'What's the matter? You look as
though someone's chasing you.'

She glanced swiftly along the corridor and grabbed Lisa by the arm,
pulling her inside.

'It's all right,' Lisa said weakly. 'I've
had news from home.'

'What's happened? Sit down and I'll

get you some water.'

She sat, unable to find the energy to stop Jane rushing around and when a glass of water was pushed into her hand she sipped it obediently.

'Now, tell me what's happened,' Jane said softly, kneeling in front of her. 'Take your time. Is it your father? Is he ill?'

'No, Dad's all right. Well, he's not ill but everything has gone and that damn Mark Treherne has got it. He's taken everything from us. Everything my family has built up and worked at for years has been spirited away.'

Sitting back on her heels, Jane studied Lisa's dark eyes and saw the despair.

'Start at the beginning and tell me everything. I don't understand what you're talking about and what has Mark to do with all this?'

Desperate to put her thoughts in order, Lisa tried to start at the beginning and work through to the telephone call from home. Slowly she began to explain her suspicions about Mark, touching briefly on his attention to her but leaving out the details.

'He was using me. Every time he spoke to me he had a motive. He tried to make out that he was attracted to me and I believed him. What a fool I've been when all the time he was trying to get information.'

Now the words tumbled out and she couldn't stop the flow.

'How could he do this to us?'

'Lisa, you're not making sense. What information could he possibly have from you that would have made any difference to the final outcome? I know how you wanted to keep control in your family but aren't you imagining Mark's rôle in this? You've cast him as the villain and I'm sure he isn't. In any case, you knew a take-over was coming up and you weren't that worried. In fact at times I thought you would be pleased when it was finalised.'

'Oh, Jane, I was sure you'd understand.'

'I do, but I also think you've worked yourself up into a fine old state.'

She got up and brought a cold sponge from the bathroom.

'Now put this over your eyes or you'll look a mess and that will make you feel worse. Now,' she continued, 'tell me honestly, it isn't the end of the world, is it? At one time you said all your financial worries would be solved if another organisation came in with you.'

'Everything we've built up has gone. It's the way it's been done and the person who is responsible that has really upset me. Our Mark Treherne is Treherne Holdings and they are now the owners.'

'I know, but if it hadn't been them it would have been someone else. The outcome would be exactly the same. Besides, at times I thought you were developing quite a thing about Mark. But look on the bright side. You were really struggling and at least you won't have the money worries.'

'I can't look at it that way. The name

will go and with it a great chunk of our lives.'

As worried as she was, she realised that the full shock hadn't yet sunk in.

'Everything is going to change.'

'I know it's no consolation to you but it's happening all the time and from what you've said no-one will actually be made redundant and financial security means a lot.'

'I suppose so.'

'At least our jobs will all be safe,' Jane said quietly.

'I don't care about that. I feel I couldn't, just couldn't work for him.'

She suddenly sensed what Jane was trying to say. Of course Andy and Jane being newly engaged would appreciate knowing their jobs were secure.

She understood but it made her feel isolated and an outsider. She was being selfish and unreasonable but she wished they'd said they wouldn't work for anyone else. It wasn't their fight and she shouldn't expect them to make a stand with her. How unrealistic and stupid she must sound. She brushed Jane's arm briefly.

'I understand,' she said quietly, 'and I'm glad you're both secure.'

She turned away, and Jane was now obviously at a loss to know what to say.

'I'm so sorry,' she said again. 'I know it's not much consolation but try not to be depressed. It might turn out better than you think.'

'I just hate him. All the holiday, he's been watching us, making notes and forming impressions. I've seen him scribbling away on the front seat. But I knew what he was doing. I had my suspicions and I was right. This makes pretty good reading,' she said, and thrust her notebook at Jane.

Looking puzzled, Jane took the book.

'What on earth is all this?'

She skimmed through some pages.

'You don't mean to say you've been monitoring him while he's been watching us. Really, Lisa, it's incredible and all this has been going on without anyone else noticing. You've really been making a report on him yourself?'

'Yes, I have,' she said defiantly and then added more hesitantly, 'I suppose you think that makes me as bad as him.'

'Well . . . '

'I know what you're thinking but honestly I had good reason. He's going to say how inefficient we are. Even the coach broke down this time and it has never happened before. He made sarcastic remarks about the video recorder and nothing has really suited him.'

'I actually think we could have done with a new coach for this journey. I know Andy's been nursing it. He's known something was wrong with the electrical system but didn't want to call a garage here because he knew it would be expensive, besides, as it was solved on the spot Mark will probably give the company a gold star for initiative.'

In spite of herself she smiled, knowing what a misery she'd been and knowing she ought to make amends.

'Oh, don't take any notice of me.'

She wanted to go now and be on her own.

'I'll get over it but at this moment I don't think I've ever hated anyone quite so much.'

On Jane's advice, she washed and made up her face afresh. Perhaps she'd been selfish to involve Jane but she had so desperately wanted to talk to someone but even now she was confused and bothered. Worse still, she didn't know where to go.

In the midst of all the muddle, a message came that there was a telephone call for her.

It had to be her father and she was determined to show him how much she was on his side. But how? And then the idea flashed again into her mind. She would say that she would make her own way back and the new owners would have to supply another driver.

It was a terrible thing to do but she needed desperate measures and this would tell everyone her family couldn't be pushed around. She sped to the booth knowing her father might not approve of her business ethics but morally she knew it would please him.

'Dad?' she asked, hoping that he wasn't feeling as depressed as the day before.

'Lisa, how are you, love?' he said quickly so no precious time was wasted. 'A lot has happened since I last spoke to you and I wanted you to know that everything is going to be all right and I don't want you to worry about a thing.'

'All right?'

She frowned and wondered what was going on.

'Yes, love. I've had a formal offer from Mr Treherne himself, in writing, and it's generous, more generous than I hoped. He must be a really nice man. I think he understands what it . . . '

'Nice!' she interrupted.

What was happening? Was everything upside down and inside out?

'What are you saying, Dad? I don't understand.'

'He wants me to continue to run

Corane Tours,' he went on as though she hadn't spoken. 'The only stipulation is that I put up the prices.'

'But you said you'd never do that.'

'Yes, I know, love, but in return we can offer better coaches and several little extras. That way we'll be much more competitive. So you see, Lisa, people will be getting more for their money. Anyway, it's all been worked out by the accountant.'

'Our coaches aren't that bad or that old,' she insisted indignantly.

'They could be a lot better but now things will improve and there's a good package for the staff. Oh, Lisa, it's such a weight off my mind. I feel ten years younger. By the way, why did you ask me about the initials? It's obviously Mark Treherne.'

'He's here, Dad. He's been on the tour, trying to find out about us,' she replied, unable to contain her anger.

'Sound man,' he said approvingly. 'Trying to find out where we went wrong, no doubt. Good idea.'

'Don't you think that it's under-handed?'

'What? Not in business. I'd have done the same thing myself.'

'You would?'

'Of course. Anyway, you tell him that I'm looking forward to meeting him in person. I must dash as it's hectic here but I wanted to tell you the latest news.'

She gulped. Her sacrifice wasn't needed. The wind had been neatly taken from her sails.

'It's great, Dad, just great.'

After a few moments she rang off. The way her father described Mark made him sound like the fairy god-mother! Surely she couldn't be that wrong about someone.

Replacing the receiver with hands that were wet and clammy with nerves, she was totally exhausted. She couldn't think any more for it was all too much. Depression, like a dark cloud gathered around her.

What a failure she was. The only thing she'd achieved was to become the odd one out and completely isolated from the others involved. Her father and friends were happy with the new arrangements. They didn't want her support and now it was herself who was slowly falling apart.

She'd never been so alone. At this minute no-one needed her and niggling at the back of her mind was the idea that her father had let her down. She'd been ready to fight and make a stand but it wasn't necessary. Everything was settled and she was the only one who was unhappy with the situation.

Aimlessly she wandered through the hotel trying to decide what to do. Deep in her heart she now knew that Mark was right when he'd said that her father's position was unchanged. Perhaps he'd been right about other things, too.

Not wanting to return to her room, she took herself outside and began the walk down the hill. Her father had called Mark a nice man and said he would have done the same thing. Had she been too harsh in her judgment, too unforgiving? Never mix business with pleasure was good advice.

Something caught the corner of her eye and looking up she saw a figure detach itself from beside a tree and come towards her. Watching Mark move nearer she reached a decision.

She must force herself to apologise. It was now or never. She had to build a bridge for herself and for everyone at Corane Tours but mostly for herself.

'Mark, I don't know what to say.'

His expression was hard.

'I've spoken to my father again and he told me about the generous package you've given him, well, for us all.'

He didn't say anything. He didn't even move but stood there while she floundered and stuttered her way through her embarrassment. She tried to explain how defensive she'd felt on behalf of her father and then this second call that caused her to think again.

Finally she stopped speaking and

hoped that he had understood for the very act of speaking had cleared her own head a little, but his expression didn't change. Looking up, she hoped for the odd flicker in his eyes but his face was set, unmoving and cold.

Then he reached into a pocket and stepped closer to her. His hand opened and something waved in front of her face, something she recognised.

With a flash of clarity she realised what they'd done to each other and that she was as bad as he was.

'You lost this?'

His tone was so cold that she shivered. He held her notebook between two fingers as though it was contaminated.

'Er, yes,' she stuttered, 'it's mine but I didn't know I'd dropped it.'

How she wished she could be casual about this but guilt was reddening her face as she remembered her notes. When had she last seen it? It was when she'd showed it to Jane. Trying to cast her mind back, she knew that she'd put it in her pocket. It must have slipped out. Maybe he hadn't read it, but looking at his eyes she knew he had and her face flamed as she thought of the comments she'd written.

There was only one hope and that was he wouldn't know it was about himself. Then, too late, she remembered the initials MT were everywhere and he would know all right.

'Quite the little spy, aren't we?'

Couldn't he understand how worried she'd been and that it made her motive more understandable?

'Although,' he repeated, 'I think Mata Hari used other methods. Perhaps you should have tried your quite delicious charms. You might be more successful.'

He thrust the book at her.

Looking at the pages, she saw that most of the comments were written in a temper or a fit of pique. Now, just when she'd been ready to make her apologies, he had found the book. Some of the notes she'd made just didn't apply now after hearing her father's latest news. She should have immediately torn them out and destroyed them. Instead what had been destroyed was their relationship, just when she'd thought something could be salvaged from the mess.

'I'm sorry,' she tried again. 'I don't know why I kept the awful thing.'

Then honesty forced her to continue.

'It was because I was so worried and I think I realised almost from the start what you were doing on this holiday.'

'But why keep this kind of diary?'

He tried to take it back but she let it fall to the ground.

'I don't know. I wanted to find out what was going on.'

'Well, you did, didn't you? You found out I came on this holiday to check for myself how the tour was run.'

Hearing him put it into words drove all thoughts of apologies away.

'So you admit it's true?'

'Up to a point,' he drawled. 'Some of it is a bit 'way out but then with your kind of imagination what can you expect?'

He was enjoying this. He was taking a

delight in seeing her at such a disadvantage. Then he shook her theory again.

'The only thing you are wrong about is the reason I spent so much time with you.'

'I know why.'

'You don't know anything. Just reading that book shows me you have the wrong idea.'

'Never!'

'Being with you wasn't anything to do with business,' he went on and his face softened. 'I wanted to get to know you. Is that so very difficult to understand?'

'You didn't want me, not the real me. You used me to find out about my father's business. That's all I meant to you.'

'You didn't listen to me before, but you'll listen to my explanation now. I admit I didn't tell you at first. After that it was too late because I knew it would turn you against me.'

'Absolutely right. It has and I'll never

forgive you, never.'

'Please forgive me,' he muttered. 'The last thing I wanted was to hurt you.'

'Oh, Mark,' she exclaimed, realising her anger had gone. 'Why couldn't we meet like two normal people without this background of intrigue?'

'It doesn't matter. Now the problems are solved and there is only you and me. I know it's difficult to understand but I had to do what I did.'

She could no longer doubt the sincerity in his voice.

'The company was losing so much money that I had to find out why,' he continued.

'But why you?'

'I'd been working hard and needed a holiday so I decided to combine business with pleasure.'

'It's right what they say, it doesn't work,' she said vaguely. 'Look what it's done to us.'

He smiled.

'I only made one mistake.'

'Mistake?' She sniffed. 'You wouldn't make a mistake.'

'I did this time. I met this girl with gorgeous hair and brown eyes and I couldn't get her out of my mind.'

'You couldn't?'

'No. This girl was unbelievable. She was lovely but drove that coach as skilfully as any man. I didn't like that for a start.'

'Tell me more about this girl.'

She wanted him to keep speaking until all her fears were driven away completely.

'She was extremely short-tempered. She was also very loyal and closed her mind to all criticisms of the family firm.'

'I'm sorry but I was so worried I could hardly think straight. You were watching everything and I didn't know what to do so I wrote it down.'

'To use in evidence against me?' he teased.

'Well, yes, maybe,' she admitted.

'Right, well, I'm withdrawing your

financial package.'

'Why? You're firing me?'

She turned away as she realised he was going to have his own back after all.

'Can't you understand what I'm trying to say?'

He pulled her close to him.

'What are you trying to say?'

'I've got another job for you.'

'Of course. You don't like women drivers. I guessed my job would go.'

'I absolutely love women drivers now.'

'You do?'

'And you are the best, but I can't bear you out of my sight for weeks at a time while you go gallivanting round Europe.'

'We don't go to that many places,' she said indignantly, hoping he would go on saying these lovely things.

'I don't want you anywhere but with me.'

'But what am I going to do?'

'Marry me, of course. What else did you think I meant?'

He sounded impatient that she hadn't understood.

'For a girl who is usually so quick on the uptake, you're slow about the things that really matter.'

'Oh, Mark, of course I'll marry you.'

Everything fell into place and the day was suddenly wonderful.

'If you miss the odd bit of driving you can take me to the office.'

'Perhaps I won't marry you after all. I might have to think about it.'

She giggled.

'No, I'm serious. I've always worked and I'm used to it.'

'You won't have time. When we have children, you can drive them to school. I'm sure you'll be very happy with that.'

'It seems,' she said demurely, 'that I shall have to settle for that if it's the best you can offer.'

'Won't it be enough?'

He kissed her thoroughly.

'There's something else you haven't thought about,' he went on.

'What's that?'

'Corane Tours will still be in the family. So now, will you marry me?'

'Oh, Mark.'

Tears filled her eyes but this time they were tears of happiness.

'That's a good enough reason to say yes.'

THE END

We do hope that you have enjoyed reading this large print book.

Did you know that all of our titles are available for purchase?

We publish a wide range of high quality large print books including:
**Romances, Mysteries, Classics
General Fiction
Non Fiction and Westerns**

Special interest titles available in large print are:
**The Little Oxford Dictionary
Music Book, Song Book
Hymn Book, Service Book**

Also available from us courtesy of Oxford University Press:
**Young Readers' Dictionary
(large print edition)
Young Readers' Thesaurus
(large print edition)**

For further information or a free brochure, please contact us at:
**Ulverscroft Large Print Books Ltd.,
The Green, Bradgate Road, Anstey,
Leicester, LE7 7FU, England.
Tel:** (00 44) **0116 236 4325**
Fax: (00 44) **0116 234 0205**

Other titles in the
Linford Romance Library:

VISIONS OF THE HEART

Christine Briscomb

When property developer Connor Grant contracted Natalie Jensen to landscape the grounds of his large country house near Ashley in South Australia, she was ecstatic. But then she discovered he was acquiring — and ripping apart — great swathes of the town. Her own mother's house and the hall where the drama group met were two of his targets. Natalie was desperate to stop Connor's plans — but she also had to fight the powerful attraction flowing between them.